Twisted Beautiee
An Erotic Thriller

Twisted Beautiee
An Erotic Thriller

BY

TRACY WILSON

http://beautifulpublications.com

Published by
Beautiful Publications LLC
Stratford, CT 06614

PRINT ISBN: 978-0-9985765-6-5
EBOOK ISBN: 978-0-9985765-9-6

Printed in the United States of America

Dedication

I dedicate this series to my alter ego, Beautiee.

'Twisted' Acknowledgements

Allow me to re-introduce myself. In the midst of all the drama in social media I thank you from the bottom of my heart.

It started out from something I knew and spun into something wild and crazy.

As I continued writing, it made perfect sense to have our cardiologists, Dr. Preston and Dr. Remi have a role in our lives... or deaths... or both – but I wouldn't stop there – I couldn't stop there... I needed more...

So I had 'messageation' with three of my favorite writers: Trinity DeKane, Tisha Andrews, and Yvonne Williams – better known as Obsession – The Pretty Writer – not to ask their permission, but to tell them they were written into this series – but the crazy doesn't stop there – this series wouldn't be complete without my brothers and sisters – so I did what had to be done... I 'Twisted' them upside down which led to more crazy...

Ooohhh... my niece and nephew fit in perfectly as if they were born for this segment in the series — and during our 'textversation' when my niece found out I fired her mother she told me... "Oh I know this is going to be good..." But that still wasn't enough...

So I went to social media and I posted a status asking for a woman to volunteer to be killed... Janet Toombs volunteered to be killed right away so I thought I was done... but then MaryJane LaRue also volunteered so another dimension was added... and 'Twisted...' but that wasn't enough...

So I kept adding... and I kept twisting... more nieces, more nephews, my aunt... my uncle... my grandparents... my husband's grandfather... and my brother-in-law...

Chapter 1

I was completely done. I was psychologically, emotionally, and physically drained. I knew I shouldn't be turning to alcohol, but it was either a drink or a shotgun and since I couldn't get my hands on a shotgun, a drink would have to do. I sat there admiring the glass of amaretto sour in front of me, picked up the cherry, and slid it into my mouth. I closed my eyes, tilted my head back slightly, and imagined the liquor going down my throat, quenching my thirst, and numbing the pain I was in. I opened my eyes and as I reached for the glass, he wrapped his hand around my hand and held the drink with me. "Who are you?" I asked as I watched him pick up the glass and take a sip with both our hands holding it…

"I'm your Thirst Quencher," he answered as we put the glass down, he leaned towards me, and began kissing me slowly and softly, sliding his tongue in my mouth, allowing me to suck the amaretto flavor. I couldn't take my eyes off of him. It was hot inside and out, and I admired the sweat dripping from his chocolate temples. We

1

picked up the glass again and he took another sip, but this time when he leaned in to kiss me he used his tongue to pour the amaretto into my mouth, sliding his tongue in a little deeper, allowing me to suck and swallow. We lifted the glass again and before he could take a sip, I brought the glass to my mouth and gulped the rest of the drink down. He looked at me with such a sad face and turned to leave but before he could, I turned him back towards me, took his face in my hands, and kissed him fully in the mouth, sliding my tongue into his so he could suck the amaretto flavor. We pulled away from kissing and I was relieved to see I changed his mind...

"Who are you?" he asked.

"I'm Beautiee," I answered as I lowered my head.

"Look at me," he whispered as he gently placed his hand under my chin and picked my head up. "What happened?"

"Long story," I answered as I tried to lower my head but couldn't. When I tried to turn my head away from him, he wouldn't allow it.

"Look at me," he whispered as he turned my head to face him. "I've got all night," he said as he looked into my face.

"I don't want to..."

"It's okay... you don't have to," he said as he stood up. "Come with me... please..." he whispered as he held out his hand. I stood up, took his hand, and allowed him to lead me to the elevator. I knew where we were going but I didn't care... I needed to numb the pain I was in and I was going to numb it one way or the other. The way I figured, this way was better than a shotgun. When the elevator doors opened, I realized where I was and started having second thoughts...

"I can't do this," I whispered as I backed up into the elevator. He stood in the door, blocking it from closing...

"Don't leave me Beautiee... please..." he whispered as he extended his hand for me to take. I took his hand again and allowed him to lead me out the elevator down the hall and into his room. Once inside, I looked around the suite, admiring the décor. The master bath was off to the right with two sinks, porcelain countertops, recessed lighting, and marble floors, and a shower built for two. The king size bed was to the left, made up with brown, cream, and red comforters and pillows. In the middle of the room was a chocolate chaise lounge, and to the right of that was a desk with a computer, a lamp, paper, pens, and a phone. "Make yourself comfortable..." he said as he sat down on his bed and patted, motioning for me to sit down next to him...

"I'd like to take a shower," I said as I opened the closet door and took the robe off the hanger.

"Whatever you want," he said, looking at me seductively.

"I need another drink" I said as I walked over to the chaise lounge and sat down.

"Amaretto sour?" he asked.

"I need something a little stronger... something to take the edge off..."

"I'll make you another amaretto," he said, completely ignoring my request. When he sat down on the chaise lounge next to me with the drink, I reached for the drink but he playfully pulled it away, smiling. "Say please..." he commanded.

"Please," I said sarcastically.

"You can do better than that," he replied just as sarcastically.

"Look," I said as I turned to face him.

"Yes Beautiee?" he said as he turned to look at me. I could tell he was really enjoying this...

"Who are you?" I asked.

"I'm your Thirst Quencher," he answered, still holding the drink...

"The ice is beginning to melt... and I'm really thirsty..."

"Here," he said as he handed me the glass and I wrapped my hand around his hand.

"Thank you," I replied, slowly taking a sip and pulling the glass away. He watched me swallow and as we both dropped the glass, he pushed me back onto the chaise lounge and began kissing me forcefully. He slowed down when he sensed I wasn't enjoying it and continued kissing me softly and sensually, sucking my tongue, tasting the amaretto. "MmmmMmmm..." he moaned between kisses, moving from my mouth to my neck...

"Don't..." I whispered...

"Please..." he panted while continuing to kiss my neck...

"I... need..." I tried to explain between kisses...

"You... need... to... let... me... be... your... Thirst... Quencher...

"Shower..." I panted...

"Okay... I'll join you..." I didn't want him to...

"No..." I panted...

"Please..."

"I'll be right back..."

"I'm... coming... with... you..."

"Okay..." I relented.

"Come with me," he said as he stood up and reached for my hand. I took his hand, stood up, picked up the robe, and let him lead me to the shower. I stepped into the bathroom and watched him come up behind me in the mirror. He unzipped my dress and began kissing my neck as he slid my dress off my shoulders and it fell to the floor. He was pleasantly surprised when he saw I was naked underneath. He quickly disrobed, dropping his clothes to the floor, turning me around to face him. His look quickly changed from seductive to hurt when he saw the bruises on my body. I tried to look away but he placed his hand under my chin, turned me to him, pulled me close to him, and kissed me. He reached to turn on the shower, took me by the hand, and led me inside. I stood underneath the water and let it soothe me as he reached for the shampoo, squirting some in his hands. He began to massage my scalp while simultaneously kissing the back of my neck...

"Mmmmmm..... That's nice..." I moaned as I began to relax...

"Ouch... what the... oh my God... Beautiee..." he whispered as he pulled his left hand away to look at the blood. I couldn't turn to look at him. I just continued to stand under the water, facing the wall, until he turned me around to face him... "Beautiee... this is glass... I need to check to see if you're still bleeding... you might need stitches... let me rinse this out... I'll try not to hurt you... be still..." he said as the shampoo ran down my head and face... "Turn your head this way... it looks like you might need stitches...

"No... I said, shaking my head.

"Let's get you cleaned up," he said completely ignoring me, until... "What are you doing?"

"What does it feel like I'm doing?" I asked him as I continued 'washing' his dick.

"It... feels... nice..." he moaned as I continued soaping him up and down. I loved watching the creamy lather run down his chocolate body...

"Ouch," I said as he started soaping my bruises...

"I'm sorry Beautiee," he whispered as he pulled me into a passionate kiss. I could feel his erection against me and I wanted him – needed him. I felt safe and secure in his arms and I wanted to stay in them for as long as I could. We stopped kissing and I wrapped my arms around him as he continued to hold me against him. "Come here," he whispered as he led me out the shower towards the bench. I sat down and he gently towel-dried my hair, being particularly careful on the left side of my head. "It looks like the bleeding stopped... you may not need stitches," he said as he continued to dry me off and then himself. When he was finished he lifted me up off the bench, careful not to grab me by my bruises, carried me to the bed, and gently laid me down on the bed. He lay behind me and pulled me close to him, spooning me, kissing me softly on my neck and shoulder...

"You... feel... so... good...," I yawned as I drifted off the sleep.

Chapter 2

"Mmmmmm....." I yawned and stretched... "Wait... what the hell... where am I... why am I naked... oh God... what happened last night?" I whispered as I started to cry... then I heard the door...

"Good morning Beautiee," he said as he came into the room with room service.

"Who are you?" I asked.

"I'm your Thirst Quencher," he answered seductively.

"My what?"

"Your Thirst Quencher," he said again as he came towards the bed...

"Why am I naked?"

"You wanted to take a shower," he whispered as he sat down close to me and started kissing me on my neck...

"Wait..."

"No..." he said playfully...

"What happened last night?"

"Here... put this on... let's have some breakfast," he said as he handed me the robe.

"Okay..." When I stood up I saw the bruises in the mirror as I was putting on the robe. I looked at him, put the robe on, and sat down to eat.

"Coffee?"

"Yes... thank you."

"When I saw you, you were in bad shape," he said as he lifted the covers off our plates. We each had scrambled eggs, bacon, home fries, toast, fruit, pastries, and orange juice.

"Where did you see me?" I asked as I ate.

"I saw you at the bar," he answered as he alternated between drinking and swallowing.

"Oh God... was I drinking?"

"Yes."

"How much did I have to drink?"

"Before I saw you... I don't know... but once I sat down and we both held the glass..."

"We both held the glass?"

"Yes..."

"That sounds nice," I said as I finished my food."

"It was... especially when you let me quench your thirst..."

"I did what?"

"We held the glass... I took a sip... I kissed you... and you sucked the amaretto off my tongue..."

"Oh wow..." I whispered, more intrigued and less afraid.

"I led you to the elevator... you didn't want to come at first..."

"How did you convince me?"

"I said please don't leave me... and you didn't..." he answered seductively.

"Is that why I'm naked?"

"No... I made you another drink... you took a sip... we dropped the glass... I started kissing you..."

"Did we make love?"

"No... you wanted to take a shower..."

"Did we make love in the shower?"

"No..."

"Why not?"

"I started to wash your hair... there was glass... there was blood...," he said as he got up and came towards me...

"What are you doing?"

"I'm checking your head," he answered as he ran his fingers through my hair, paying close attention to the left side of my head...

"That hurts," I whispered...

"I'm so sorry Beautiee...," he whispered as he started kissing me on my neck...

"Did you hurt me?" I asked tearfully.

"Beautiee..." he answered with hurt and anguish on his face... "I could never hurt you... I love you..." he answered as he leaned in to kiss me...

"You love me?"

"Yeeesss... Beautiee... I love you..." he moaned as he continued kissing me softly...

"So... who hurt me then?" I asked with tears in my eyes...

"I don't know who hurt you..." he said as he laid me back on the bed, opened my robe, and climbed on top of me... "But I swear on my life... when I find out... he's a fuckin' dead man..." he growled as he spread my legs...

"Don't..." I whispered as he continued kissing me...

"Please... I love you... Don't you want me?"

"I'm scared..."

"I know..."

"Please don't..."

"Okay... I'll stop... if that's what you want..." he panted as he kissed me fully in the mouth while sliding his right hand across my breasts...

"Mmmm..."

"Do you still want me to stop?" he asked as he slid down and began sucking my right nipple while caressing my left breast...

"Oooohhh...."

"So you don't want me to stop... I didn't think so..." he panted as he began swirling his tongue around my left nipple while caressing my right breast. I lifted my head slightly and started trembling as he slid his hands under the small of my back. Lifting me up...

"I'm scared..."

"Don't be... I won't hurt you... I promise..." he moaned as I felt his breath between my legs...

"You promise?"

"Proommmmmisssseeee..."

11

"Ohhh.... Yeeesss...." I moaned as he buried his face between my legs and began licking, sucking, and slurping... "Stop..."

"Am I hurting you?"

"No..."

"Then why?"

"I don't want to cum..."

"Why..." he panted as he slowed down but didn't stop completely...

"Because... I won't cum again..." I breathed...

"I'll make you cum as much as you want..."

"Promise?"

"Promise... now where was I..."

"Ooohhh... right there..."

"Yeesss... right here..."

"Don't stop... I'm cumming!" I screamed as I arched my back up off the bed, trembling as he continued licking, sucking, and slurping...

"Mmmmmm.... You taste delicious..." he said as he stood up and began taking off his clothes. He looked so good standing there completely nude, chiseled in all the right places. He stood there and smiled, allowing me to admire his body, stroking his dick slowly, hypnotizing me. As he approached the bed, I slid down to the edge and hesitated before taking his dick in my mouth...

"Beautiee..." he moaned as I took his dick all the way in my mouth, down my throat, then slowly pulling it back out, swirling my tongue around it as I did so, then taking it back in my mouth again... Stop..."

"Did I do something wrong?" I asked as I looked up at him while continuing to lick his dick...

"No Beautiee... you did everything right," he panted as he pushed me back a little and stood away from me. "Move back, he commanded. I did as I was told and he sat in front of me on the bed, spreading his legs. "Come sit here," he commanded, motioning for me to sit on his dick.

"Oooohhh..." I moaned as I slid onto his dick all the way down to his balls...

"Come here," he commanded as he pulled me close to him and began stroking me, holding me and kissing me passionately...

"Mmmmmm.....   Mmmmmm.... Mmmmmm...." I moaned as I squeezed him tighter. He felt so good... his dick was amazing... he was giving me life... and he was making me cum... "Shit..." I moaned as I closed my eyes, tilted my head back, braced myself, and enjoyed the ride...

"Fuck..." he moaned as he squeezed me harder, burying his head in my neck...

"Yyyeeesss..." I moaned, wrapping my arms around his neck...

"I'm cummmmmmiiinnng!" he growled...

"I'm cmmmmmiiinnng with you!" I screamed as we came together. We began kissing each other, taking turns sucking each other's tongues, and holding each other as our orgasms transcended from our bodies to our hearts...

"I love you Beautiee..."

"I love you too... Thirst Quencher..."

"I guess I should tell you my name," he laughed.

"Thirst Quencher..." I sighed as I lay my head on his shoulder..."

"Bazil... my name is Bazil..."

"Thirst Quencher..." I repeated as I pulled him into a kiss...

"As... much... as... I'm... enjoying... this..."

"Yyyeeeesss..."

"We... need... to... check... out..."

"I... don't... want... to... check... out..."

"You... want... more..."

"Yyyyeeesss... please..." I breathed as he began thrusting...

"Mmmmmm...."

"Yyyyeesss.... right... there..."

"Oooohhh...."

"Fuck... ooohhh... sshhhiiittt..." he growled as he grabbed me up and laid me down in one quick motion...

"Oooohhh.... yyeeesss... harder..."

"Is... that... what... you... want?"

"Oooohhh... God.... Yyyeeesssss!" I screamed as he threw my legs up on his shoulders and continued thrusting...

"Uuuggghhh... uuuggghhh... uuuggghhh... uuuggghhh!" We continued to lay there, panting, and kissing for a few minutes...You... got... some... good... pussy..."

"You... got... some... good... dick..." I sighed...

"Indeed..."

"It's... been... so... long..."

"So long for what?" Dick?"

"Yes... and no..."

"What then?"

"It's been so long since I've felt good..."

"It's... been... my... pleasure... to... make... you... feel... better..."

"Mine too..."

"Marry... me... Beautiee..."

"Whhhaaattt???"

"I... said... Marry... me..."

"Wait... are... you... serious?"

"Yeeesss... Beautiee..."

"But... MmmmMmmm..." I moaned as he kissed me deeper, purposely covering my mouth with his, swirling his tongue around mine so I couldn't object..."MmmmMmmmmm..." I moaned as he started thrusting again...

"Mmmmmm....." he moaned as he started thrusting harder and deeper...

"Mmmmmm..... Mmmmmm..... Mmmmmm....." was all I could do and all I wanted to do as he continued thrusting because he never let up, his mouth was still covering mine, his tongue was still deep inside, and I was cumming again...

"Mmmmmmph...   Mmmmmmph... Mmmmmmph..."

"Mmmmmm...   Mmmmmm... Mmmmmm..."

"Is... that... a.... yes...?"

"I... want... to... but..."

"Beautiee?"

"Yes?"

"You just said it's been a long time since you've felt good right?" he asked as he propped himself on his arm beside me while caressing me...

"Yyyeeesss..."

"So..." we started kissing again... "Marry... me... and... if... you... do... I promise... I'll make you feel good... everyday... for the rest of your life..."

"Okay... I'll... marry... you..."

"Did you just say yes?"

"Yes my Thirst Quencher... I said yes... I'll marry you!"

"Beautiee... I love you..." he whispered with tears in his eyes..."

"I love you too... now let's plan a wedding!" I yelled as I jumped out of bed.

Chapter 3

"Easy Beautiee," he laughed as he jumped up out the bed after me and grabbed me from behind, kissing me on my neck..."Go get in the shower... I'll see you when you get out..."

"Aren't you coming with me?" I pouted.

"I'd love to join you... but I have something I need to take care of... and I need to do it quickly so we can check outta here on time," he answered as he picked up his cell phone.

"Okay my Thirst Quencher," I said as I ran off to jump in the shower... and Bazil picked up his cell phone...

"Hey..."

"Bazil... I miss you..."

"I found her..."

"Are you sure?"

"I've never been more sure of anything in my life..."

"I wish I didn't have to share you..."

"Don't start that shit again Trevor..."

"I'm sorry... I can't help it..."

"I'm hanging up..."

"Please don't... tell me about her..."

"Her name is Beautiee..."

"Does she live up to her name?"

"She's beyond her name..."

"Damn... I don't stand a chance do I?"

"Trevor... you never did...

"Bazil... please... don't say that..."

"Look Trevor... I love you... you know that... but I told you what it was from the beginning..."

"How am I supposed to live without you?"

"Here we go again with the fuckin' dramatics..."

"Bazil... please..."

"You know what – fuck this – I'm done with your ass..."

"You'll never be done with me Bazil... that's why you put up with me... that's why you love me... you may have found the one... but deep down... I'll always be the one..."

"She's absolutely the one Trevor... she's everything I've been looking for and longing for..."

"Oh... I get it... you finally got some pussy so now you're in love..."

"Fuck you Trevor!"

"Soon my love... so tell me... when will I get some pussy..."

"NEVER! I'll kill you first!"

"Damn... that good huh?"

"Yyyyeeeessss..."

"So you think she'll be down with us? Remember what happened with the last one...

"That was unfortunate..."

"You loved her too Bazil... and she left you... they all leave you..."

"She didn't leave me Trevor..."

"What do you mean Bazil?'

"I couldn't let her leave me..."

"Bazil... please tell me you didn't..."

"I did... and if Beautiee ever tries to leave me... I'll do it again..."

"Bazil... you're scaring me..."

"Don't be scared Trevor... I'd never hurt you... unless you make me..."

"You don't wanna do that Bazil..."

"Oh please... I'm not worried about you Trevor..."

"You think you have it all figured out... you think you're invincible..."

"I am invincible... and as long as you continue to do my bidding... you'll be just fine Trevor..."

"So you still want my ass... I knew it..."

"Absolutely... I'll see you soon... I just need to marry Beautiee first..."

"WHAT?! MARRIED?! Are you fuckin' kidding me? Where does that leave me?"

"Trevor... nothing has to change between us..."

"You're getting married Bazil... that changes everything..."

"We can still be together Trevor..."

"How can we be together when you have a wife?"

"You're my best friend Trevor... Beautiee will never suspect a thing..."

"And here I was thinking you were breaking up with me..."

"I need you to do something for me Trevor..."

"Anything for you Bazil..."

"I'm serious Trevor..."

"Aaiight, Aaiight... what do you need me to do?"

"I need you to pull the surveillance video from the Hotel Zero Degrees in Stamford."

"Stamford, Connecticut?"

"Yes... copy it, send it to my phone, and then make it disappear..."

"Bazil... what did you do?"

"Something happened here last night... something bad..."

"She doesn't remember a thing does she?"

"No she doesn't... and I pray she never remembers..."

"You've done this before... why do you care if she remembers?"

"I didn't do this Trevor... somebody else did..."

"So why should I erase the footage then?"

"Because I was in the lobby..."

"So what? You didn't do anything... right?"

"No I didn't... but someone did... and once they see the footage they'll look for witnesses..."

"Bazil... let me get a hold of the security footage... you might be in the clear... then you can let the police handle this and you're your hands can stay clean..."

"I can't trust amatures... besides... I made Beautiee a promise..."

"Bazil! Have you lost your fuckin' mind?"

"I haven't lost my mind Trevor... I've lost my heart..."

"Bazil..."

"Trevor – just do it!"

"Bazil... Baby... listen to me... please..."

"What Trevor?"

"Let me get the footage and review it, then I'll send it to you... if you still feel like you need to take care of him, then I'll help you... but promise me you won't do anything without talking to me..."

"I promise you... I won't do anything without talking to you first... in fact... I may call you so you can hear all the gory details..."

"Bazil!"

"He hurt her... bad..."

"Damn... what happened?"

"I didn't know she was bruised when I undressed her..."

"Damn... she was that easy?"

"Don't talk about her like that... she's not a whore..."

"How can you be so sure?"

"When we got in the shower... there was blood and glass in her hair..."

"Oh shit! What the fuck happened?"

"That's what I need you to tell me..."

"Okay Bazil... I'll get right on it... and I'll get back to you."

"Thank you Trevor... oh... Trevor?"

"Yes Bazil?"

"Find out if Beautiee had a room at this hotel... and if she did... take care of it."

"Got it... talk to you in a bit."

Chapter 4

"Your turn!" I squealed as I ran up behind Bazil and began kissing him on his neck...

"Beautiee... sit down... we need to talk..."

"Is everything okay?" I asked, praying that he wasn't about to change his mind...

"No..."

"What's wrong?"

"I want to give you the most beautiful, romantic wedding your heart desires..."

"I don't care about that my Thirst Quencher..."

"But I do... and I want our wedding day to be special..."

"It will be..."

"While you were in the shower... I was thinking... How would you feel about getting married in Vegas?"

"You're not going to believe this..."

"Believe what?"

"That's where we said we were getting married..."

"We?"

"Yes... We weren't really getting married in Vegas... we just said we were because we didn't want anyone on our honeymoon."

"Umm... What?"

"Let me explain..."

"Please..."

"I told my best friend I was getting married..."

"Okay..."

"So... her husband said they would join us and be our witnesses..."

"Sounds good..."

"Yea... I thought so too... until he said he was going to take the entire week off and stay on our honeymoon with us..."

"Oh hell no!"

"Exactly!"

"What the hell is wrong with him?"

"He didn't see anything wrong with it... he tried to convince me that they'd stay in a different hotel and they wouldn't bother us..."

"That's crazy..."

"They took another couple with them on their honeymoon and they all went camping... my best friend told me she heard everything they were doing in their tent..."

"Waiiiittt....," Bazil laughed... "Tents?"

"Yes..."

"So... if she heard everything..."

"So did they..."

"Damn... your friend's open..."

"I know..."

"So where did you end up getting married?"

"It wasn't in Vegas..." I sighed.

"Did you want to get married in Vegas?"

"Yes..."

"Well then... I'll go get in the shower... and you sit here... go on the computer... and pick out whatever you want," he said before he pulled me into a kiss...

"Okay my Thirst Quencher," I beamed. I watched him turn to go towards the bathroom and got turned on again by the sight of his ass... "Le'me get on this computer," I said out loud as I turned it on and went to littlechapel.com/wedding-packages. I went to the Chapel of the Flowers and looked at the packages and chose the Cherish package. The silk flower petals, roses, bouquet, and boutonniere were stunning. The package also included photography, a wedding coordinator, a wedding planner, live music, round-trip limousine service for the bride, a separate limousine for the groom, hair and make-up, a VIP Consultation Service to the Reginal Justice Center to obtain your marriage license, and a video of the ceremony. I went to look at the venues and immediately fell in love with the Magnolia Chapel. I was mesmerized by the marble mosaic floors, crystal chandeliers, light gray shimmering wallpaper, crystal beaded curtains, dual glass mirrored silver pillars, elegant candelabras, and custom blush benches with leather finishes. I logged into my account at hotes.com and looked at all the hotels with 5-star ratings. I kept scrolling and clicking... and then I found it... the Four Seasons Hotel. "This is the one," I said out loud as I looked at the pictures of the Presidential Suite. The views of Vegas were breathtaking from all the windows of the room and the master bathroom was the most elegant I'd ever seen. I nearly fell out of my chair when I saw $3,000 per night...

"Hey...," he said as he caught me.

"Hey...," I sighed.

"Find everything you want?"

"Yyyyeeeessss...," I moaned.

"Okay... here... take this," he said as he handed me a Black American Express Card... "and book it while I get dressed..."

"Wait..."

"What's wrong Beautiee?"

"I can't..."

"You can't marry me?"

"Yes... I can marry you... but..."

"Come here Beautiee," he said as he patted the bed for me to sit next to him. "Talk to me...," he pleaded.

"I can't wear that dress..."

"The dress from last night?"

"Yea..."

"Here... put this on... I hope you like it... it's all I could find on short notice," he said as he handed me the bag and I took out the clothes..."

"Oooohhh... I hope these fit me..."

"If they don't, we'll go get you something that fits," he smiled.

"Okay," I squealed as I jumped up off the bed and reached for the red underwear. I loved the way he was looking at me as I put them on.

"They look good on you," he said seductively.

"They feel good too," I said just as seductively.

"Let me help you with that," he said as I tried to reach for the bra. I stood still as he came up behind me and held the bra for me to put my arms through the straps and as he got closer to my shoulders, he began messaging my breasts while kissing me on the back of my neck...

"Oooohhh... that feels so good... my Thirst Quencher...," I moaned as he moved up to my earlobe while continuing to massage my breasts...

"Let me close this for you," he said as he pulled up the straps and clasped the bra. "Perfect," he said lovingly.

"These fit perfectly... how did you know my size?" I asked as I pulled up the jeans..."

"I got to know your body intimately," he answered as he pulled me into a kiss...

"Mmmmmm...," I moaned...

"Here," he said as he pulled the blue shirt over my head and pulled it down.

"Thank you," I whispered.

"You're welcome... put on the socks and sneakers," he said as he picked up the phone... "Yes... we need a later check out... 3pm... okay... thanks...

"What about my hair?" I asked.

"Let me look at you," he said as he ran his fingers through my hair... "Does it still hurt?"

"A little..."

"Leave your hair down then... Let's get this booked... we can leave tonight..."

"Tonight?"

"Yes Beautiee... if that's okay with you..."

"Yyyyeeessss...," I sighed.

"Good... let's do this," he said as he sat down beside me and looked at my choices..."Oh wow... this is really beautiful... I had no idea..."

"Me either..."

"I can't wait to marry you Beautiee..."

"I can't wait either my Thirst Quencher...," I sighed.

"Okay... it's all set... we just need to book our flight..."

"Can we go first class?"

"Of course... let me see," he said as he was looking at priceline.com..."Perfect... this flight leaves at a little after 10 tonight and we can be in Vegas tomorrow morning..."

"Okay...," I sighed.

"Done! Let's go Beautiee," he said as he opened the door for me...

"Wait... your card..." I said as I ran back to pick it up, looked at it, and read his full name: Bazil J. Osgood.

Chapter 5

Once we got to the airport and went through check in, I was elated to get on the plane. It was a breeze because we were only wearing what we had on and we had no luggage to check in. Bazil tried peeking over my shoulder without being obvious, but it didn't work...

"What are you looking at Beautiee," he asked me, as if he didn't already know what I was doing...

"What size are you?"

"What size do you think I am...," he asked seductively...

"I'm not talking about your dick," I laughed...

"Well shit... I am... what size are ya?" she laughed. I could tell she had a few too many so I wasn't going to get into a confrontation... but I was definitely going to answer her question...

"He's about the size of this bottle here... would you like to feel it or you gonna take my word for it?"

"Shittt... I ain't had no dick in a while... I might wanna feel that shit," she laughed...

"As you wish!" I said as I stood up and swung the bottle... right into Bazil's hand...

"Give me that," he laughed...

"Get your lady," she laughed...

"See... I was trying to be a gentleman... you know what... never mind... here Beautiee... handle your business!" he said as he handed me back the bottle...

"Well Bitch... whatchu' goin' do?" she slurred...

"I'ma handle my business... like he said," I laughed as I put the bottle down, reached between Bazil's legs, and started massaging his dick...

"Awww shit... y'all 'bout to be in the mile high club," she laughed...

"You wanna?" Bazil asked...

"Hell yea!" I said as we got up out our seats, went into the bathroom, and locked the door... "Drop your pants," I panted... Bazil didn't hesitate... "This is gonna be good," I said as I took his dick in my hand... "But it has to be quick," I said as I started sucking...

"Beautiee...," he moaned as he ran his fingers through my hair before grabbing the sides of my head, pushing his dick further into my mouth... "Oh shit... I'm about to bust my nut... Beautiee...," he moaned as he shot his creamy goodness into the back of my throat... "Easy... I'm a little sensitive..."

"Okay...," I whispered...

"Drop those pants... and bend over...," he commanded. As soon as I did as I was told, he slid inside me and I had to brace myself on the sink to keep from falling... "Bazil... Bazil... Bazil...," I panted as he grabbed a hold of my waist and began thrusting harder and deeper...

"Cum for me Beautiee...," he growled...

"Bazil...," I panted, turning on the blower to muffle our sounds...

"Cum for meeee...," he growled, covering my mouth...

"MmmmMmmmMmmmMmmmmm!" I screamed into his hand while his creamy goodness ran down my legs...

"Everything okay in there?" the stewardess asked as she knocked on the door...

"Everything's fine!" I answered as we cleaned ourselves up, made ourselves presentable, and went back to our seats...

"Congratulations," the stewardess whispered in my year...

"Thank you," I laughed... "Now... what size are you?" I asked Bazil...

"I'm a size 13..."

"Okay," I said as I completed my purchase of the Modern Prong Wedding Band in 14k White Gold from zoara.com. Bazil completed his purchase of the Elegant Shared Prong Diamond Wedding Ring in 14k White Gold for me as I drifted off to sleep. When we woke up, it was time for us to get off the plane so we got up out our seats, waited for the stewardess to open the door, and we walked off hand-in-hand. After we got our bags, we got in the limousine, and went straight to City Hall.

Chapter 6

"Good afternoon..." the clerk smiled... "How may I help you?"

"We're here to get our marriage license..." I said as I smiled...

"Aww... congratulations..."

"Thank you..."

"Do you have valid identification?"

"We have valid identification..." Bazil said as he showed the clerk his driver's license...

"May I have your ID please?" she asked me...

"Sure..." I said as I handed her my license...

"I need to make a copy of these to attach to your application – I'll be right back..." she said as she walked over to the copy machine. Bazil and I looked at each other and smiled...

"Here ya go..." the clerk said as she gave us back our licenses...

"I need you both to fill this out completely – once you fill it out – I'll look it over, make sure it's filled out properly, and then we'll all sign it..."

"Okay…" Bazil said as he took the form and began filling it out. I waited patiently as he filled out his side, but I wanted him to hurry up so I could fill out mine…

"Here, here!" Bazil laughed as he gave it to me. I studied his side and then started filling out my side with my name, date of birth, social security number, etc., and then I filled in the rest of the form: Mother – Connie Thompson, Father – Jake Thompson, City of Birth – Mt. Vernon, State – NY, Prior Marriages – No, Maiden Name – Beautiee Thompson, Name on Marriage Certificate –Beautiee Osgood

After I filled in the name to be put on the Marriage Certificate I checked 'no' where they asked for preference to hyphenate the name. I saw Bazil's signature at the bottom of the form and I started crying after I signed my name…

"Aww…" the clerk said as she handed me tissues…

"Sorry…" I laughed…

"Don't ever apologize for happiness…" she said as she took the form and read it over…

"Bazil?" she asked…

"Yes?"

"Did you fill this out of your own free will?"

"Yes Maam…"

"Is this your signature?" she asked as she pointed to his signature…

"Yes Maam…"

"Beautiee?"

"Yes?"

"Did you fill this out of your own free will?"

"Yes Maam!"

"Is this your signature?" she asked as she pointed to my signature...

"Yes Maam!"

"Okay..." she laughed as she signed the form. "I'm going to process this and get you your license – once I do that – you can get married - I'll be right back..." she said as she went into the office behind the counter...

"I love you Bazil..."

"I love you too..." Bazil said and then he kissed me...

"Here's your license..." the clerk said as she handed us our license. We looked at the license, and then we looked at each other...

"Do you have any questions?" I looked at our license again and read the signature at the bottom:

Prepared by: Roselle DeNino
Title: City Clerk
City: Las Vegas
State: NV

"No..." I sighed...

"Do you have any questions Bazil?"

"No Maam..."

"After you get married I'll sign it, date it, and then I'll mail it out to Vital Records for

Nevada. You'll receive your Marriage Certificate from the Vital Records Office..."

"Thank you Ms. DeNino..." I said as I gave her a hug..."

"You can call me Roselle..." she said as she pulled us both into a hug and started crying...

"You okay?" Bazil asked...

"I'm fine – I'm just happy..." she said as she wiped her eyes..."

"Aww... we're happy too... right Beautiee?"

"Yessss..." I breathed...

"Okay – I'm going to head on over to the Magnolia Chapel – I'll see you soon..." Roselle said as she left. We went outside, got back in the limousine, and headed to Kay Jewelers...

Bazil got out, extended his hand, helped me out, and we both went inside...

"Good afternoon – welcome to Kay Jewelers – my name is Jack ‑ how may I help you?"

"We're here to pick up our wedding rings..." Bazil answered...

"May I please have your name?"

"Bazil Osgood..."

"Mr. Osgood! We've been expecting you – you're here to pick up the Modern Prong Wedding Band in 14k White Gold and the Elegant Shared Prong Diamond Wedding Ring in 14k White Gold – right?"

"Yes – that's right..."

"Come with me..." Jack said as he came out from behind the counter and escorted Bazil behind the counter and into the back room. I waited for them to come out and Jack put the rings on the counter in their boxes so we could see them in the light...

"Beautiee... what do you think?" I didn't answer him... I took his face in my hands and kissed him hard...

"Oh my – you must really love your rings!" Jack laughed...

"I really love our rings... and I really love him..." I said as Bazil smiled...

"You wanna try them on?"

"I dunno..." I sighed...

"Why not?" Bazil asked...

"I might not want to take it off..."

"I understand – we have another set in the case over here if you'd like to see how it'll look on your hand...

"No – I wanna try on our rings!" I squealed...

"Changed your mind huh?" Bazil laughed...

"Yea..." I sighed...

"Give me your hand..." Bazil said. I gave him my hand and I started shaking as he put the ring on my finger...

"It's perfect..." I sighed as I looked at my hand...

"It looks really great on you..." Jack said...

"Give me your hand Bazil..." I said. Bazil gave me his hand and I took my time putting the ring on his finger...

"Beautiee..." he breathed as he kissed me...

"You like it?"

"I love it... you have exquisite taste..."

"I agree – you do have exquisite taste – maybe I'll be so blessed one day..." Jack said...

"You will..." I said...

"From your lips to God's ears – let me get these in a bag for you so you can go get married – congratulations!"

"Thank you..." we both said in unison. Bazil took the bag, took my hand, we got back in the limousine, and headed straight to David's Bridal...

Bazil got out, extended his hand, helped me out, and we both went inside...

"Good afternoon – welcome to David's Bridal – my name is Jessica – how may I help you?"

"We're here to pick up my tuxedo and her wedding dress..." Bazil answered...

"Congratulations! May I have your names?"

"Thank you – I'm Bazil Osgood and this is Beautiee..."

"Mr. Osgood – we've been waiting for you to get here – would you like to try on your tuxedo?"

"Do we have time?"

"We'll make time..."

"I don't wanna be late for our wedding..." I sighed...

"Where are you getting married?"

"At the Magnolia Chapel..."

"Oh don't worry – they won't start without you – I'll call Roselle and let her know you're here..."

"Thank you Jessica – I appreciate it..."

"I know you're in a hurry – I just wanna make sure everything fits perfectly..."

"What if it doesn't?" Bazil asked...

"We have what you ordered in stock – if it doesn't fit, we'll just re-size you..."

"Thank you Jessica..."

"You're welcome – Beautiee – I'm going to ask you to wait here – okay?"

"Okay... I guess..."

"I don't want you to see him before the wedding – and I don't want him to see you either..."

"Oh – okay!" I squealed...

"C'mon Mr. Osgood – I can see how excited she is!" Jessica laughed as she took Bazil in the back. I sat down and waited for about 15 minutes or so and then I saw them heading to the front with a couple of bags...

"Ohhh... can I see?" I asked...

"No..." Bazil answered as he pulled me into a kiss and held the bag away from me...

"Okay..." I sighed...

"C'mon Beautiee – let's go get you into your gown – we'll be right back..." Jessica said as she took me by the hand and we hurried to the back... "Your dress is already in the dressing room – go try it on – I'll come in when you're ready..."

"You can come in now if you want..." I said...

"You want me to come in? Now?"

"Yea..."

"Okay – sure..." Jessica smiled as she came in the dressing room with me...

"I can't believe I'm doing this..." I sighed as I took off my clothes and put on the dress...

"You're not sure you wanna marry him?"

"Hell yea I'm sure – but we've only known each other since last night..."

"What? Oh my God!"

"We met last night at the hotel... I went to his room... we took a shower together... and then we went to sleep..."

"Aww... that sounds nice..."

"He asked me to marry him this morning after we made love... and I said yes..."

"Aww... that's beautiful..." she said as she started crying...

"This dress... is beautiful... too..." I said as I cried...

"Okay... c'mon... we'll never get you outta here like this..." she laughed as we hugged each other...

"I can't wait for him to see me in this dress..." I sighed...

"I'm so happy for you... thank you for sharing with me..."

"You're welcome..." I said as she helped me take off the dress and we put it in a bag...

"Okay – we're ready – let's go up-front to your husband..." she said as she took the bag, took me by the hand, and we hurried to the front of the store... "Everything you need is in there – congratulations – now go get married!"

"Okay..." Bazil laughed as he took my hand, we went outside, got back in the limousine, and headed straight for the Magnolia Chapel...

"Thank God – c'mon!" the stylist said as she took me by the hand and led me away from Bazil into another room...

"C'mon Mr. Osgood..." the 2nd stylist said as he took Bazil by the hand and led him into the other room...

"Beautiee – we're gonna get you dressed – and then we'll do your hair and make-up..." the stylist said as she took my dress, shoes, etc. out the bag...

"I'm going to do your hair and make-up..." another stylist said as she came over to me, held up my face by my chin, turned my head left and right, and went over to the make-up...

"Go light on the make-up..." I said...

"Good idea — less is more — especially 'cause you're already pretty..." she said as she looked through the different foundations...

"Aww... thank you..."

"You're welcome — take off your clothes..."

"Okay..." I laughed as I got up, took my clothes off, and sat back in the chair...

"How would you like to wear your hair?"

"I'd like to wear it down..."

"Okay — I'll give you some curls to accentuate your face..." she said as she styled my hair and put in the Classic Pave Crystal Floral Comb... "How's this?" she asked...

"I love it..." I whispered as I started crying...

"Uh uh — we can't have that — you can't cry until after I've done your make-up — and make sure you dab with tissues — don't wipe — you don't wanna smear your make-up — we need you to look good for your pictures..."

"Okay..." I sniffed. I sat still until I finished my make-up and then I got up to look in the mirror...

"Is that light enough for you?"

"Yes... thank you..."

"You're welcome...Congratulations..." she said as she started to leave...

"Wait..."

"Yes?"

"What's your name?"

"Linda..."

"Thank you Linda..."

"You're welcome..." she said as she left...

"Ready for me now?" the 1st stylist laughed...

"Yesss....." I breathed...

"Okay – let's get you dressed..." she said as she helped me put on my Floral Beaded Lace & Tule Mermaid dress. Once I got my dress on she helped me step into my Pearlized Platform Sandals with Scalloped Edges...

"Oh my God..." I whispered...

"Uh uh – stop that – you don't have any tissues!" she laughed...

"You're right – what's your name?"

"Lori..."

"Thank you Lori..."

"You're welcome – wait here..." she said as she left the room...

"I'm Carl – I'll be helping you get ready for your wedding..."

"Thank you Carl..."

"Do you need me to help you get undressed?"

"I've been dressing and undressing myself for a long time now..." Bazil laughed...

"I'm sorry..."

"Don't be – it was funny..."

"Oh my goodness..." he said as he pulled the Wilke Rodriguez Black Satin Edged Notch Lapel tuxedo out the bag..."

"I take it you like my tuxedo..."

"I love it! I plan on getting married in this same tuxedo one day..."

"Are you engaged?" Bazil asked as he started getting dressed...

"I haven't met my wife yet... but I will..."

"Yes... you will..."

"Look at you!" Carl said as he took Bazil by the shoulders and put him in front of the mirror...

"I look good..."

"You certainly do..."

"Is he ready?" Lori asked as she stood outside the door...

"He's ready..."

"Okay – c'mon Mr. Osgood..." she said as she took Bazil by the hand and escorted him to where Roselle was waiting...

"Where's my bride?"

"I'll get her right now..." Lori said as she left Bazil standing there and came to get me... "Okay Beautiee – let's go!" she said as she extended her arm so she could escort me down the aisle. I could hear the orchestra playing, 'So Nice To Be With You' by Smokey Robinson on violins and I started to cry...

"Uh uh – you don't have any tissues!" Lori whispered as she handed me a tissue and I dabbed my eyes and walked into the room...

"Beautiee..." Bazil whispered as I started walking down the aisle. I tried not to cry but I couldn't help it. When I got to where Bazil was standing, Bazil took my face in his hands, kissed me, pulled me close to him, and we started dancing... "I love you..." Bazil whispered as tears streamed down his face...

"I love you too..."

"You look beautiful..."

"So do you..."

"I can't believe we're getting married..."

"Neither can I..." Roselle and Lori watched as we looked into each other's eyes and danced until the song was over. When the orchestra stopped playing we started kissing...

"Beloved..." Roselle laughed as she interrupted us... "We are gathered here this afternoon to join Beautiee Thompson and Bazil Osgood in marriage. You have both come before me and expressed your desire to become husband and wife. Do you have rings?"

"Yes – we have rings..." Bazil said as he took two ring boxes out his pocket...

"Okay – take the rings out the boxes – Beautiee – you take his ring – Bazil – you take her ring..."

"Okay..." we both said in unison as I took his ring and he took mine...

"Okay – Beautiee – do you have anything you want to say to Bazil?"

"Yes I do..." I answered as I took his hands... "Bazil... my Thirst Quencher... my love... if anyone ever told me that not only would I meet the love of my life, but that I'd also be marrying him... I wouldn't have listened to them or believed them," I said as I started to tear up... "You saw me at my worst and chose me in spite of what you saw... you comforted me... you loved me... and you made me feel something I haven't felt in a long time... you made me feel good. When you came to me... you gave me life and you saved my life... I love you sooo much... and I promise to love you forever," I said as I cried. Bazil didn't wait for Roselle to ask as he responded to me...

"Beautiee... my love... I've been looking for you forever," Bazil said as he teared up... "And I never thought I'd find you," he said as he broke down crying. Roselle was crying along with us both as she handed us tissues. After Bazil composed himself he continued... "I knew I loved you from the moment I saw you... even in your darkest place you were beautiful to me... I know

I'm your Thirst Quencher... but Beautiee... you are also my Thirst Quencher," he said as he started tearing up again... "When you chose me you also gave me life and saved my life... I love you Beautiee... thank you for choosing me," he said as he cried...

"Bazil – put the ring on Beautiee's finger – and repeat after me..."

"Okay – I'm ready..." Bazil said...

"Beautiee – I take you as my wife, with your faults and your strengths, as I offer myself to you with my faults and my strengths..." Bazil repeated after Roselle and then she continued... "I will help you when you need help and turn to you when I need help. Today - I choose to spend the rest of my life with you..." I started crying as Bazil repeated the vows to me. When he was finished, I took his face in my hands and kissed him... Roselle waited for us to finish kissing and then she continued...

"Okay Beautiee – put the ring on Bazil's finger - and repeat after me..."

"Okay – I'm ready..." I said...

"Bazil... My Thirst Quencher..." I said... and then I started crying. Bazil took his hands, touched my face, and started crying as I continued... "I take you as my husband, with your faults and your strengths, as I offer myself to you with my faults and my strengths. I will

48

help you when you need help and turn to you when I need help. Today – I choose to spend the rest of my life with you..."

"I love you so much Beautiee..." Bazil breathed as he kissed me hard...

"I love you too..."

"By the power invested in me by the State of Nevada – I now pronounce you husband and wife!" Roselle said as Bazil pulled me to him and we held each other, kissing feverishly... "Ummmm... your limousine is waiting to take you back to your hotel..." she laughed...

"I love you Mrs. Osgood..."

"I love you Mr. Osgood..."

"I can't wait to get back to the hotel..."

"Neither can I..."

"We'll be in touch with you when your video and pictures are ready..."

"Thank you – come with me Mrs. Osgood!" Bazil said as he took me by the hand, escorted me out to the limousine, made sure I got in, and got in beside me. We started kissing again and didn't stop until we got to the hotel...

"We're here..." the driver said...

"Come with me Mrs. Osgood..." Bazil said as he opened the door, got out, and extended his hand to help me out the limousine...

"Coming Mr. Osgood..." I beamed as I took his hand and got out.

"Congratulations!" the driver said as he took off. Bazil took my hand and we walked into the hotel lobby to the elevator and took the elevator to the Presidential Suite. When we got off the elevator, I started to walk but Bazil stopped me...

"Wait a minute..." he said as he opened the door to the room... "Come here..." he said as he picked me up, carried me into the room, and laid me on the bed... "Welcome to Vegas Mrs. Osgood..." he said as he laid down on top of me and began kissing me fully...

"Mmmm..." I moaned as he moved down to my neck and shoulders...

"Beautiee..." he breathed in my ear as he slid my dress down my body...

"Oh Bazil..." I moaned as he took my breasts in his hands and began licking and sucking my nipples. I ripped his shirt open and grabbed his back, digging my nails into his lower back as he moved down to my stomach. He stood up, slid the dress off me, and looked at me lovingly while taking off his clothes. I watched him get completely naked and he stood there for a few moments, allowing me to admire his gorgeous erection, before he walked towards me...

"Thirsty?" he breathed...

"Yes my Thirst Quencher..." I answered as I pulled him closer so his erection could reach my mouth...

"Beautiee..." he moaned as I took him into my mouth completely, looking up at him to make sure he was watching me, and he was...

"I'm thirsty too..." he moaned before pulling out of my mouth and climbing on top of me...

"Bazil..." I moaned as he slid inside me...

"Yes... Beautiee..." Bazil moaned as he started thrusting...

"Ohh... Ohh... Ohh... Bazil..." I moaned as he started thrusting deeper...

"Ummph... Ummph... Ummph... Ummph..." Bazil moaned as I spread my legs wider and grabbed his back, pushing him in deeper...

"Mmmm... Mmmm... Mmmm..." I moaned in Bazil's mouth as he smothered me with deep kisses...

"Mmmph... Mmmph... Mmmph..." Bazil moaned in my mouth as he braced himself up with his hands and continued thrusting...

"Oh shit... Bazil... I'm cumming..."

"I'm cumming with you..."

"Bazil..."

"Beautiee..."

"Bazil..."

"Beautiee... Uuuggghhhh!"

"Baaazzziiilll!" I screamed as he thrust harder...

"Damn Beautiee..." he breathed as he laid down on top of me and kissed me... "You want more... don't you?"

"Yes Bazil... yes... but let's go in front of the window..."

"Okay..." Bazil breathed as he got up, picked me up, and carried me to the window... "What do you want?" he asked as he bent me over, kissing me down my back...

"I want you Bazil..." I breathed..."

"Here? In front of the window?"

"Yes Bazil... Yes..." I breathed as he slid inside me again... "Bazil... Oh God!" I moaned as I braced myself on the window sill and Bazil grabbed me by my waist as he continued thrusting...

"Is this what you want?"

"Yes Bazil..." I moaned...

"Oh shittt... damn..." Bazil breathed...

"Fuck me Bazil...Oooohhh!"

"Uuugh! Uuugh! Uuugh!" Bazil growled as he slowed down, kissing me on my neck...

"Bazil..."

"Beautiee..." Bazil breathed as I felt his cum dripping down my legs. Bazil stopped, pulled out of me, turned me to face him, and held me... "I love you Mrs. Osgood..." he said as he kissed me...

"I love you too Mr. Osgood..." I said as I kissed him back...

"Come with me..." Bazil said as he took my hand and led me to the shower. Bazil turned on the water, and then came up behind me. We both admired our bodies in the mirror as it steamed up, and then Bazil started kissing me...

"Let's get in the shower..." I said as we moved into the shower while continuing to kiss...

"Mmmm..." Bazil moaned as he reached between my legs and began playing with my pussy while continuing to kiss me...

"Mmmm..." I moaned as I reached down to grab his dick... "Wait..." I breathed as I pushed Bazil away so I could sit down on the bench. After I sat down, I pulled Bazil towards my mouth again and began sucking him as the water beat down on us...

"Oh Beautiee..." Bazil moaned as he began massaging my head through my hair with his hands, steadying himself so he wouldn't come out my mouth. I could tell he was about to cum as his legs started trembling and he grabbed my head, pushing his dick further down my throat... "Aaaagggghhhh!" he yelled as I swallowed his warmth... "Easy Beautiee..." Bazil panted. I slowed down but didn't stop right away. When I did stop, I pulled him to my face by his ass and looked up at him as he looked down at me while playing with my hair... "Cumere..." he said as he pulled me up to stand in front of him... "Hold on..." he commanded as I grabbed the bars on both sides of the bench. Bazil squatted down so his face was directly in front of my pussy, placed my legs on his shoulders, and buried his face in my pussy...

"Oh Bazil..." I moaned as he slid his tongue in and out...

"Bazil... Bazil..." I moaned as he moved his tongue under the hood of my clit... "Bazil... Bazil... Bazil..." I moaned as Bazil started sucking my clit ferociously... "Bazil... I'm cumming... I'm cumming... I'm cumming!" Bazil continued sucking and slurping as my legs shook and clamped around his head...

"Mmmm..." Bazil moaned as he let my legs down...

"Bazil..." I moaned as he pulled me into a kiss and slid inside me before I realized he was erect again... "Ooohhh..." I moaned as I wrapped my arms around his upper body to brace myself...

"Ummph... Ummph... Ummph..." Bazil growled as he grabbed my upper body, pulled me closer, and continued thrusting...

"I'm cumming again... Oooohhhhh...."

"Ummph! Ummph! Ummph!" Bazil growled as he buried his head in my neck...

"Ohh... Ohh... Ohh... Baazziilll!!"

"Aaaaggghhhh!" Bazil growled as we both came..."

"Beautiee..." Bazil moaned in my ear...

"Bazil..." I moaned as I pulled him into a kiss...

"Mmmm... Yesss..."

"We better hurry up and finish before they run out of hot water..." I laughed...

"Okay..." Bazil agreed as we got got out the shower, put on our robes, and walked hand-in-hand back to the bedroom...

"I'm hungry..." I breathed...

"Give me a minute..." Bazil laughed...

"I need to eat..."

"Ooohhh... Okay... let's look at the menu..." he said as he went over to the table, picked up the menu, and sat on the bed... "Hmmm... let's start with the Antipasto Assorted Cheese, Charcuterie Meats..."

"Okay..." I agreed as I sat down on the bed next to him, took his dick in my hand, and started stroking it...

"Mmmm... that feels nice..."

"It does..."

"We can also get a cheese plate – Artisanal Cheeses with Seasonal Accompaniments..." he breathed...

"Mmmm... that sound's good..." I breathed as he got harder in my hand and I continued stroking him...

"That feels... good..." he breathed...

"What else can we get to eat?"

"This... looks... good..." he panted...

"What?"

"Two Tuxedo Strawberries..."

"Le'me see..." I breathed as I continued stroking his dick and he showed me the menu...

"I want the Double Chocolate Brownies and Blondie Cake Pops..."

"Mmmm.... Shit... Okay..."

"Ooohhh. Let's get the Sin City Angus Burger – it comes with Bacon, Avocado, and White Cheddar – and Fries..."

"Okay – that's it!" Bazil growled as he turned around, grabbed me by my shoulders, flipped me on my back, spread my legs, and thrust himself inside me...

"Bazil... Huh... Huh..."

"Uggh! Uggh! Uggh!"

"Huh! Huh! Huh!"

"Uggh! Uggh! Uggh!"

"Huh! Huh! Huh!!"

"Uggh! Uggh! Uggh!"

"Fuck me... I'm cumming... I'm cumming..."

"Uggh! Uggh! Uggh! Uuuggghhhh!" Bazil collapsed on me and kissed me hard...

"Mmmmm..." I moaned as I opened my mouth and we started tonguing each other down...

"I'm going to order room service now..."

"Okay..." I breathed as we continued kissing...

"We'll eat in our dining room..."

"Okay..."

"When we're done eating... we'll go sit in the living room..."

"Okay..."

"And I'll make you an Amaretto Sour..."

"Okay..."

"And... after you drink it... I'll suck your tongue..."

"Huh... Okay..."

"Let me go Beautiee..."

"No..." I breathed as he tried to get up but I locked my legs behind him...

'Okay..." he said as he reached over and picked up the phone...

"Room Service..."

"Hello... I'd like to place an order..." he said as I pulled him back down and kissed his neck...

"Yes Mr. Osgood – what can we get you?"

"Mm mm..." Bazil moaned as I grabbed his ass and pushed him back inside me... "I'll have the Antipasto Assorted Cheese and Charcuterie Meats..."

"Okay..."

"I'll also... have... the Artisanal Cheeses with Seasonal Accompaniments..."

"Okay..."

"Uggh..." Bazil moaned as he started stroking me slowly... "Two Tuxedo Strawberries..."

"Okay..."

"Uggh... Double Chocolate Brownies and Blondie Cake Pops..."

"Okay – anything else?"

"Yeesss... two Sin City Burgers..."

"Okay Mr. Osgood – it'll be about 45 minutes – is that alright?"

"That's fine..." he grunted as he hung up and then started thrusting harder and faster...

"Oohh... Oohh... Oohh... Oohh..."

"Uggh! Uggh! Uggh! Uggh!"

"Damn Bazil... you're fuckin' me so good... huh..."

"Uggh! Uggh! Uggh! Uggh!"

"Fuck me Bazil..."

"Uggh!"

"Aahh!"

"Uggh!"

"Aahh!"

"Uggh!"

"Aahh!"

"Uggh!"

"Aahh!"

"Uuuggghhhh!"

"Aaaaaahhhhhh!"

"Mrs. Osgood..." he breathed as he kissed me...

"Yes... my Thirst Quencher?"

"Is this what I have to look forward too?" he asked as we continued kissing...

"Mmmm... Hmmm..."

"Mmmmm..." he moaned...

"Bazil..." I breathed...

"Yesss... Beautiee..."

"Can... we... talk?" I asked between kisses...

"Yes... we... can... talk..."

"Bazil... stop..."

"No..." he breathed as he pushed his tongue in my mouth...

"Mmmmm...."

"Mmmmm..." Bazil moaned as he climbed on top of me... spread my legs... and I pushed him off me gently...

"Beautiee... you don't want me?"

"Hell yea... I want you..."

"Then why..."

"Because... I can't..." I tried to say as he climbed back on top of me and started kissing me again... "I want... to... talk..."

"Okay... we'll talk... and then..." he breathed in my ear as he kissed my neck and shoulders... "we're fucking..." he said as he started kissing me again... "Do you understand?"

"Yes... Yes my Thirst Quencher..." I breathed as he kissed me fully...

"Okay..." he said as he turned on his side, propped himself up on his elbow, and looked down at me... "Let's talk..."

"I love you..."

"I love you too..."

"Can I ask you something?"

"Of course..."

"I've never felt like this..." Bazil smoothed my hair away from my face and smiled...

"I know..."

"You're so good..."

"I know..."

"We're you always this good?" Bazil bust out laughing...

"Aaahaaaa! Aaahaaaa! Aaahaaaa!"

"I shouldn't've asked..."

"Beautiee..." he laughed... I'm not laughing at you... but..." he said as he laughed again... "I just can't believe you asked me that!" he laughed...

"I'm sorry..."

"Don't be sorry..."

"Okay..."

"I started having sex when I was 16..."

"Okay..."

"My father and I had open communication when it came to sex..."

"That's good..."

"My father told me the key to getting pussy was simple..."

"He did?"

"He said all I had to do was listen..."

"That's it?"

"My father told me listening was the best thing I could do if I wanted pussy – mind you – I was only 16 at the time – so I wasn't sure what he meant – so I asked him what he meant..."

"What'd he say?" I asked as I propped myself up on my elbow...

"My father asked me if I ever heard him having sex with my mother..."

"Really?"

"I told him I heard them sometimes and he asked me what I heard..."

"Oh my God! What'd you say?"

"I told him I heard moaning..."

"You weren't embarrassed?"

"I was – but my father said it was okay to be embarrassed – and then he asked me what I thought when I heard them moaning..."

"What'd you say?"

"I told him I thought it must feel good and he said that's exactly the point ˗ when you're having sex, you listen to her moaning – if she's moaning, that means she's enjoying it – and as long as you make sure she's enjoying it you'll always get pussy..."

"Wow!"

""So did your parents talk to you about sex?"

"My father wasn't around when I was growing up. My mother talked to me about my period and using birth control, but she never talked to me about sex the way your father talked to you..."

"So you couldn't talk to her when you started having sex?"

"I thought I could... but when I told her I was having sex, she slapped me..."

"Oh my God! Why?"

"I'm not sure..."

"Maybe she thought you were too young..."

"I guess..." I sighed...

"Did you ever hear your mother having sex?"

"Yea..." I sighed as I looked away from Bazil...

"Beautiee..." Bazil said as he picked up my face by my chin...

"Yes Bazil?"

"What happened?"

"I was 15..." Bazil didn't say anything. He lay down on his back, pulled me up under him, and held me as I laid my head on his chest. I took a deep breath and then I continued... "It was about 3 in the morning..."

"Go on..."

"I had to pee..."

"Okay..."

"I had to walk past my mother's room to get to the bathroom..."

"Ooohhh..."

"I heard them having sex so I tip-toed past her room and went to the bathroom... when I finished, I tried to tip-toe back but she came out her room..."

"Was she mad?"

"Yea..."

"What happened?"

"She asked me what I was doing so I told her I had to go to the bathroom... but she didn't believe me..."

"She really thought you were lying?"

"She called me a Sneaky Bitch..." I sighed...

"Beautiee..."

"I went back to bed and when we got up later in the day... she told me I was going to live with my grandfather..."

"She really sent you to live with your grandfather? All because she thought you were listening to her have sex?"

"Yes..." I whispered...

"Beautiee... I'm sorry..."

"Don't be – I was happy to go..."

"You were?"

"Yea..."

"I'm glad that made you happy..."

"I loved my grandfather..."

"Aww..."

"I always called him Daddy..."

"Did you think he was your father?"

"No – I called him Daddy because he was the only father I had when I was little..."

"That's sweet..."

"My mother hated it..." I laughed...

"You did it on purpose – didn't you?"

"No..."

"Your grandfather never corrected you?"

"He did..."

"But you still called him Daddy?"

"Yea..."

"You were really close huh?"

"Yea..."

"What about your grandmother – where you close with her?"

"Yea – Grandma was cool..."

"Cool?"

"Yea – I could talk to her about anything..."

"Really?"

"Yea..." I laughed... "I remember I went to her house one day and she had company so I was sitting quietly listening to their conversation and they were talking about how horny they get when they have their periods..."

"What's so funny about that?"

"I jumped in the conversation and said I know – right?"

"Oh shit!" Bazil laughed...

"What was your first time like?"

"It was awkward – but she didn't know that..."

"She didn't?"

"Nope – I just remembered what my father said, took my time, and got the pussy..."

"I wish I was that girl..." I sighed...

"You're first time wasn't special?"

"No – he was a fuckin' jerk!"

"How old were you?"

"I was 16..."

"I'm sorry..." Bazil said as he kissed me...

"My husband never made me come..."

"Oh shit! Never?"

"Never..."

"So you didn't enjoy it?"

"I enjoyed it up until he came..."

"That's selfish..."

"As soon as I started coming he would come... and then he'd go to sleep..." I sighed...

"Did he ever go down on you?"

"No..."

"Did you suck his dick?"

"Yea..."

"Selfish mutha fucka..."

"When was the first time you ate pussy?"

"In my 20's – when was the first time you sucked dick?"

"I sucked my boyfriend's dick in high school..."

"I wish I was your boyfriend in high school..." Bazil sighed...

"Me too..."

"You ever do 69?"

"No..."

"You wanna do 69?"

"Yea..."

"You wanna be on top?"

"No..."

"You sure?"

"Yea..." I breathed as Bazil ran his hand down my body, between my legs, and spread my lips...

"Ooohhh..." I moaned...

"You're wet..."

"Yeesss..." I moaned as he slid his fingers in and started swirling them around...

"Oooohhh..." I moaned again. Bazil got up on his knees, came towards my head, straddled my head, and put his dick in my mouth. I opened my mouth a bit more, lifted my head a little, and started sucking...

"Oh shit... Beautiee..." Bazil moaned before he held my legs apart and dove in...

"MMMMM! MMMMM! MMMMM!" I moaned on his dick as my body shook and I began experiencing multiple orgasms...

"MMMPH! MMMPH! MMMPH!" Bazil moaned as he quickened his pace and began fucking my mouth harder as his body trembled and I grabbed his ass and squeezed it...

"MMMMMMMMMMM!" I moaned on his dick as I arched my back and rose up off the bed...

"MMMMMPPPHH!" Bazil moaned as he came in my mouth and I held him by his ass as I swallowed...

"MMMMM... MMMMM... MMMMM..." I moaned on Bazil's dick as he continued licking, sucking, and slurping, giving me mini orgasms...

"Yes Beautiee... suck it... shit..." he moaned as he started fucking my mouth again and went back to licking, sucking, and slurping while turning me on my side...

"HMMMM... HMMMM... HMMMM... HMMMM... HMMMM..." I moaned as my legs trembled and I came again...

"MMMPH! MMMPH! MMMPH! MMMPH! MMMPH!" Bazil moaned as I pushed his dick in deeper, swallowed, and sucked harder. Bazil and I let go of each other and lay on our backs as I panted...

"That... was... so... fucking... good!"

"Yes... it... was... intense..."

"I... came... so... hard..."

"Me... too..." Bazil said as he turned himself right-side up and propped himself up on his elbow beside me...

"I loved that..." I breathed...

"So did I..."

"Can we do it again?"

"We can do it..." he said as he kissed me... "As much... as... you... want..."

"Somebody's at the door..." I said as I sat up...

"Hold on!" Bazil said as he jumped up, threw on his robe, and went to the door...

"Room Service!"

"Come on in..." Bazil said as the server came in with the serving cart...

"Shall I put this on the table for you?"

"No thank you..."

"Please sign here..."

"Okay..."

"Congratulations..."

"Thank you... good night..." Bazil said as he closed the door and came back into the bedroom... "Mrs. Osgood – please come with me..."

"Yes Mr. Osgood..." I beamed as I got up outta bed. Bazil held open the robe for me so I could put it on and then he pulled me into a kiss...

"I love you Mrs. Osgood..."

"I love you too..." I breathed. Bazil let go of me, took me by the hand, led me into the dining room, pulled out the chair for me to sit down, and then sat down across from me where the food cart was...

"Oh my God – there's so much food!"

"We've worked up enough of an appetite to handle it..." Bazil said as he put all the food on the table...

"Are you going to talk to our son the way your father talked to you?" I asked as we started eating the Antipasto Assorted Cheese, Charcuterie Meats..."

"Absolutely..."

"What if we have a girl – will you talk to her too?" I asked as I we put some Artisanal Cheeses with Seasonal Accompaniments on our plate and continued eating...

"Absolutely – I'll probably talk to her more..." he answered as the put the Tuxedo Strawberries on our plate...

"Me too - those look good..."

"I agree..." he agreed as we continued eating...

"Will you talk to our son?" he asked as he put the Double Chocolate Brownies and Blondie Cake Pops on our plate...

"Of course!"

"Just checking..." he laughed...

"Oh my God – these are sooo good!" I said as I tasted the brownies...

"You're right – they are good..." he agreed...

"I'm not sure what I'll say to our daughter though..."

"Why not?"

"I can talk to her – but how do I tell our daughter to make sure the dick is good?"

"You tell her the same thing I'm going to tell her..."

"What are you going to tell her?"

"I'm going to tell her to make sure she has a man that listens..." he answered as he started eating the blondie cake pop..."

"Aww... I love you..." I said as I put the blondie cake pop in my mouth...

"I love you too..."

"Have you always wanted children?" I asked as I picked up the Sin City Angus Burger and took a bite...

"Yes..." he answered as he picked up his burger and took a bite...

"Me too..." I said as I finished my burger and started my fries. We continued eating until we were finished and then Bazil spoke...

"Come with me..." he said as I stood up and he led me over to the Chaise Lounge in front of the window... "Lay down..." he commanded. I did as I was told and watched him go to the bar and make an Amaretto Sour. Bazil came back over to the lounger, sat down beside me, and passed me the glass... "Drink..." I took a sip; Bazil kissed me, and sucked the Amaretto off my tongue... "Mmmm..." he moaned. Bazil took a sip and kissed me again, this time allowing me to suck the Amaretto off his tongue...

"Mmmm..." I moaned. We continued taking turns, sipping, drinking, and sucking each other's tongues, until the glass was empty...

"You like cumming with my dick in your mouth... don't you?"

"Yesss..."

"I can tell when you're ready to cum... you start sucking my dick harder..."

"You like that?"

"Hell Yea!" he breathed... "What makes you wanna suck my dick?"

"I love making you feel good..."

"Aww... I love you..."

"I love it when you grab my head play in my hair, and talk dirty when I suck it..."

"Oh yea?"

"Yea..."

"I love tasting you..."

"You do?"

"Hell yea – you taste good, you get wet, and you quench my thirst..."

"I taste good?"

"Hell yea..."

"Aww... thank you..."

"You're welcome..."

"It feels so good..." I breathed...

"You're imagining me sucking your pussy right now... aren't you?"

"Yeesss...."

"Close your eyes..."

"Okay..." I breathed...

"Slide down in the chair a little..."

"Okay..."

"Spread your legs..."

"Okay...

"Keep your eyes closed... and imagine me sucking on your pussy..."

"Huh... Bazil..."

"Touch yourself..."

"Bazil..." I moaned as I started rubbing my clit..."

"Keep your eyes closed... and imagine my tongue going up and down..."

"Ohhh.... Ooohhh..."

"Imagine my tongue fucking your pussy..."

"Bazil... Huh... Fuck..." Bazil got up, came up towards my face, and startled me by putting his dick in my mouth...

"Keep your eyes closed..."

"Mmmm.... Mmmm...." I moaned as he fucked my mouth slowly...

"Imagine me sucking your clit while you're sucking my dick..." he whispered as he grabbed my head and pushed his dick in my mouth further...

"Hmmmm.... Hmmmm.... Hmmm...." I moaned on his dick as I started cumming...

"Yes... that's it... imagine yourself cumming... in my mouth... as I'm cumming... in yours!" he growled as we both came simultaneously...

"MMMMM... MMMMM... MMMMM... MMMMM... MMMMM!"

"UUUGH! UUUGH! UUUGH! UUUGH! UUUGH! How'd that feel?" he asked as I took his dick out my mouth, opened my eyes, and looked up at him...

"Fuck me..." I breathed...

"Is that what you want?" he asked as he looked down at me...

"Yes... my Thirst Quencher..." I breathed as I stood up...

"Come with me..." he said as he took me by the hand, led me to the bed, pushed me down onto the bed, climbed on top of me, eased himself inside me, put his tongue in my mouth, covered my mouth with his, and fucked me for the rest of the night.

Chapter 7

"Good morning..." Bazil mumbled as he answered the phone...

"Good morning Mr. Osgood..."

"Who is this?" Bazil asked as he sat up...

"I'm sorry – this is Leonard – I'm calling from the Spa..."

"What can I do for you Leonard?" Bazil yawned...

"I was calling to schedule your All-Over-Elegance package..."

"Excuse me?"

"At the time of your booking, you selected the All-Over-Elegance package from the Spa..."

"Oh... I see... hold on... Beautiee?"

"Yes Bazil?" I yawned...

"This is Leonard – he's calling to schedule our All-Over-Elegance package..."

"Oh wow – you want me to talk to him?"

"No – I'll talk to him – go ahead Leonard..."

"Okay – the All-Over-Elegance package includes a 50-Minute Four Seasons Custom massage, a 50-Minute Pure Results Facial, an 80-Minute Dessert Detox Wrap, a 50-Minute Four Seasons Signature Manicure, and a 75 Minute Four Seasons Signature Pedicure..."

"I have no problem spending a day at the spa – but I'm not getting a manicure or a pedicure..." Bazil laughed...

"I can assure you Mr. Osgood – we don't paint your nails and toes..." Leonard laughed... "In fact – we do lots of manicures and pedicures for men – one of our best customers is Smokey Robinson..."

"Is that right?"

"Yes sir – he's very meticulous in his appearance – he knows the ladies love it..."

"Hmmm... okay... I'll do it... especially because it'll make my wife happy..." he said as he pulled me into a kiss..."

"I love you..."

"I love you too..."

"Okay Mr. Osgood – since you'll be spending the day with us – let's get you booked today – how's 1:00?"

"He wants to book us for 1:00 – is that okay with you?"

"That's fine..." I sighed...

"Okay – we'll see you both at 1:00 – oh – before I forget – are you comfortable with a man massaging your body?"

"To be honest... I never thought about it..." Bazil laughed...

"Most of the time the wives don't want another woman touching their husbands and vice-versa..." Leonard laughed...

"I definitely don't want another man feeling all over my wife..." Bazil laughed...

"Okay..." Leonard laughed... "We'll see you at 1 p.m...." he said and then he hung up...

"What time is it?" I asked...

"It's a little after 9..." Bazil answered as he pulled me back down on my back and climbed on top of me...

"I'm hungry..." I breathed...

"So am I..." he breathed as he started kissing me...

"I need coffee..."

"I need pussy..." he breathed as he eased himself inside me and put his tongue in my mouth...

"Mmmm... Mmmm... Mmmm... I moaned in his mouth...

"Mmmph... Mmmph... Mmmph..."

"Mmmm... Mmmm... Mmmm... Mmmm..."

"Mmmph... Mmmph... Mmmph... Mmmph..." Bazil flipped us over so he was on his back, I was on top of him, and he grabbed my ass and pushed me down on his dick...

"MMMM! MMMM! MMMM! MMMM!"

"MMMMPH! MMMMPH! MMMMPH! MMMMPH!" We continued kissing as Bazil held me until our orgasms subsided...

"I love morning sex…" I breathed…

"Me too…"

"I need coffee now…"

"Okay – I'll call room service…" he said as he reached for the phone…

"Thank you for calling the Veranda – good morning Mr. Osgood – what can we get you for breakfast?'

"How'd you know it was me?" Bazil laughed…

"Your name and room number comes up when you call…"

"Oh… I see – well we need coffee…"

"Yes please…" I agreed…

"Would you like juice as well?"

"Orange juice?"

"Sure – we can do that – what else would you like – we have a breakfast buffet, omelets, or light and fresh…"

"Hmmm… I'm pretty hungry…"

"I'd suggest The 'Hash' – Two Eggs, Slow Braised Beef Short Ribs, Roasted Potatoes, Sweet Peppers, and Onions…"

"I'll take that…"

"I don't want the beef short ribs – do they have another choice?" I asked…

"We have 'The American' – Two Eggs, Choice of Breakfast Meat, Hash Browns, and Choice of Toast…"

"I'll take it!" I exclaimed…

"Okay – how would you like your eggs?"

"Scrambled..." Bazil answered...

"Okay – we'll get that up to your room in about 15 minutes..." the hostess said and then she hung up...

"Doesn't give us a lot of time..." Bazil said as he jumped up and hurried to the bathroom...

"What's your hurry?" I laughed as I followed right behind him...

"I had to pee..." he laughed...

"Me too..."

"We can have coffee, eat breakfast, have juice..."

"And then go back to bed..." I interrupted...

"We can do that..." he breathed as he pulled me into a kiss...

"Bazil... stop..." I breathed as he put his hand between my legs and started playing with my clit...

"Is that what you want?"

"No..."

"I didn't think so..."

"I just... don't... wanna... get... interrupted..."

"Room service!"

"Hold on!" Bazil yelled as he threw on his robe and hurried to get the door...

"Thank you..." he said as he opened the door..."

"Shall I bring this inside for you?"

"Sure..." Bazil answered as he opened the door and the server pushed the breakfast cart into the dining room...

"Enjoy your breakfast..." he said as he turned to leave, and then he left...

"You can come out now..." Bazil laughed...

"Good..." I said as I put on my robe, came out, and sat at the table...

"Here..." Bazil said as he handed me a cup of coffee...

"Mmmm... I needed this..." I breathed as I drank...

"Is that all you need?" he asked as he made himself a cup of coffee...

"You know better than to ask me that..." I laughed...

"Tell me anyway..."

"I need you... My Thirst Quencher..." I said as I put my coffee down, got up, went over to him, opened my robe, straddled him, and sat on his dick...

"Oh yea?" he breathed as he grabbed my ass and started moving me back and forth on his dick...

"Yeeesss..." I moaned...

"You need to finish your coffee... before it gets cold..." he breathed...

"I can't reach it..." I breathed...

"I'll get it..." he breathed as he reached for my coffee and handed it to me...

"Mmmmmm.... I love drinking coffee... like this..." I breathed as I rode his dick...

"So do I..." he breathed as he sipped his coffee...

"I wonder if we can eat like this." I breathed...

"I don't think so..." he breathed... "We'd end up making a mess...

"I'm cumming..." I moaned as I put my cup down...

"I'm cumming with you..." he growled as he grabbed my ass and held me down on his dick as I rode faster...

"HAAAH! HAAAH! HAAAH! HAAAH!"

"UUUGH! UUUGH! UUUGH! UUUGH!"

"That's it..." I breathed... "I want my coffee like that from now on..."

"Me too..." he breathed as he held me and kissed me...

"We better eat before our food gets cold..."

"Okay..." he said as he let go of me and I got up and sat beside him...

"I loved that..." I said as I started eating...

"So did I..."

"I still need you..."

"I still need you too..."

"I want to go back to bed..."

"So do I..."

"I hope I can stay awake..."

"Me too..." We finished eating without speaking. When I was done, I got up from the table, went over to the bed, pulled back the covers, and climbed in...

"Hey..." Bazil said as he climbed in bed beside me and pulled me into a kiss...

"Hey..." I yawned as we both fell asleep.

"Good morning..." Bazil answered...

"Good afternoon Mr. Osgood..."

"Afternoon? Oh Shit – what time is it?"

"It's 12 p.m."

"Oh thank God – I thought we were late..." he laughed..."

"Not at all – this is why we give all our clients a call 1 hour before their scheduled appointment..."

"What's your name?"

"I'm Melanie..."

"Thank you Melanie..." Bazil said and then he hung up... "Beautiee..."

"Huh?"

"It's 12 – we gotta get up and get in the shower..." he said as he got up and went into the bathroom...

"Okay..." I said as I got up out the bed and followed him into the bathroom, went up behind him, and started kissing him on his neck...

"Beautiee... we need to be downstairs at 1..."

"I know..." I breathed as I turned him to face me and threw my arms around his neck...

"Come with me..." he said as he pulled me into the shower, turned on the water, and pulled me underneath the water as he started kissing me. Bazil backed me into the corner and I wrapped my legs around him and wrapped my arms around his neck as he eased himself inside me and started thrusting...

"Hmmph! Hmmph! Hmmph!"

"Mmmph! Mmmph! Mmmph!"

"Hmmph! Hmmph! Hmmph!"

"Mmmph! Mmmph! Mmmph!"

"Hmmph! Hmmph! Hmmph!"

"Mmmph! Mmmph! Mmmph!"

"Hmmph! Hmmph! Hmmph!"

"Mmmph! Mmmph! Mmmph!"

"Hmmph! Hmmph! Hmmph!"

"Mmmph! Mmmph! Mmmph!"

"Hmmph! Hmmph! Hmmph!"

"Mmmph! Mmmph! Mmmph!"

"HMMPH! HMMPH! HMMPH!"

"MMMPH! MMMPH! MMMPH!"

"HMMPH! HMMPH! HMMPH!"

"MMMPH! MMMPH! MMMPH!" We continued kissing for a few moments, took our showers, got out, dried off, and went back into the bedroom...

"I wonder how we're supposed to dress for this..." I laughed...

"I don't think it really matters – I'd say dress causal – they're just gonna have us take all our clothes off anyway..."

"You're probably right…" We finished getting dressed, picked up the keys, and headed downstairs…

"Mr. & Mrs. Osgood – right this way…" Leonard said as we followed him into the spa…

"Mr. & Mrs. Osgood – welcome to the Four Seasons Spa – you'll be happy you chose the All-Over Elegance package – it will leave you breathless…"

"You're Melanie – right?" Bazil asked…

"Yes – I'm Melanie – I'll be taking care of your wife – and Leonard will take care of you…"

"Hi Melanie – will we both be in the same room?"

"Yes Mrs. Osgood – come with me – we need to get you undressed so you can get into your robes – after you get into your robes, we'll get you over to your tables, you'll lay down on your stomach, and we'll put you to sleep…"

"Oh so we put the robes on backwards?" Bazil asked…

"Yes Mr. Osgood…"

"Okay – I'm ready…" I breathed.

"So am I…" Bazil breathed.

Chapter 8

When we were done with our pedicures we both walked out of the spa with our robes on and slippers that showed off our toes... "That color looks good on you..."

"Thank you..." I sighed...

"Did you enjoy your services today?" Melanie asked...

"Yesss..." I sighed...

"Mr. Osgood? How was everything?" Leonard asked...

"Better than I expected..."

"That's great to hear!"

"If it weren't for my wife, I' probably never get a massage or a facial – let alone a pedicure..." Bazil laughed...

"Do you see yourself coming back in the future?"

"Absolutely..."

"That's great – I'm glad you're pleased..."

"I am Leonard..."

"What should we do now?" I asked...

"My advice is to do nothing for at least an hour or so..." Melanie answered...

"Why's that?" Bazil asked...

"You just had a wonderful experience – go upstairs to your room and relax – let your body absorb the minerals and essential oils..."

"Okay..." I sighed...

"C'mon Mrs. Osgood..." Bazil said as he put his arm around me, I put my arm around him, and we walked arm in arm to the lobby. When we got in the room, Bazil didn't wait... "I've been waiting to do this since you stepped out..." he said as he pulled me close to him, pulled me into a kiss, and pushed my robe off my shoulders...

"Mmmm..." I moaned as I pushed his robe off his shoulders...

"What do you want?"

"You..."

"As you wish..." he said as he picked me up, carried me to the bed, laid me down, lay down on top of me, and eased himself inside me...

"Ohhhh... Bazil..."

Yes... Beautiee..."

"Huh... Huh... Huh... Huh..."

"Uggh... Uggh... Uggh... Ugh..." I pulled Bazil down, grabbed his ass, and pushed him in deeper...

"You want it?" Bazil growled as he started pounding my pussy...

"Yes! Oh God! Yes! Fuck me! I'm Cummiinnnggg!"

"Uuugh! Uuugh! Uuugh! Uuugh! Uuuugggghhhh!"

"Mr. Osgood..." I breathed...

"Yes... Mrs. Osgood..."

"I need to find out what minerals and essential oils they used..."

"Why?"

"So I can rub you down every night..." I breathed as I pulled him into a kiss...

"Mmmm..." he moaned as he kissed me back... "I'd like that..."

"We can put it in the bath water..."

"Indeed..."

"I wanna ride your dick in the tub..."

"We don't have to wait for that..."

"We don't?"

"We can do that here..."

"Mmmm..."

"You want more?"

"Yeesss...."

"Come with me..." he said as he got up and held out his hand to help me up. I took his hand, got up off the bed, and followed him into the bathroom. I sat on the bench as Bazil ran the water until the tub was full... "Mrs. Osgood?"

"Yes Mr. Osgood?" I answered as I stood up. Bazil took my hand, led me to the tub, stepped in, sat down, and leaned back in the tub. I stepped in the tub, sat on his dick, wrapped my arms around his neck, and started riding his dick as he held me... "Huh... Huh... Huh... Huh..."

"Yes Beautiee... that's it... ride my dick... fuck..."

"Huh... Huh... Huh... Huh..."

"Uggh... Uggh... Uggh... Uggh..."

"Aaagh... Aaagh... Aaagh... Aaagh... Aaaagggghhhh!"

"Uggh Uggh! Uggh! Uggh! Uuuugggghhhh!

"Fuck!"

"Fuck!"

"We got water all over the floor..."

"That's what towels are for..." Bazil breathed as he pulled me into a kiss...

"I love you..."

"I love you too..."

"The water's starting to get cold..."

"C'mon..." Bazil said as he held on to the sides of the tub and lifted us up... "Let's get outta here – I have a surprise for you..." he said as he stepped out of the tub and helped me step out of the tub...

"Ooohhh... where is it?" I asked as I threw my arms around his neck...

"Let's go to bed..." he answered as he pulled me into a kiss...

"Okay!" I squealed as I ran out the bathroom, into the bedroom, and jumped on the bed...

"I guess you're excited..." Bazil laughed as he jumped on the bed beside me...

"Can I have my surprise now? Please?"

"What's in it for me?" Bazil asked as he pulled me down on the bed and lay down on top of me...

"Anything you want..." I answered as he put my hands above my head and held them above my head...

"Anything?" he asked as he started tickling me...

"Yes!" I laughed... "Anything!"

"Okay..." he said as he kissed me... "I'll tell you... but remember... you owe me..."

"Okay..." I agreed as I sat up...

"Tonight... we're going to dinner... we're going to have drinks... and we're going dancing... at the Beauty & Essex Marquee Night Club..."

"Oh Bazil!" I squealed as I jumped on top of him, straddled him, and kissed him all over his face... "Go look in the closet..." I jumped up off him, ran to the closet, and snatched the door open...

"Oh my God! When did you do this?"

"I did this before we got on the plane..."

"How?"

"When you were in the shower, I went on the computer got the tickets, and then I went downstairs and bought a couple of outfits..."

"So you had these all along?"

"I had them all along..." he answered as I started to cry...

"Beautiee..." he whispered as he got up off the bed, came over to me, and held me...

"I love you so much..." I sniffed...

"I love you too..." he breathed as he kissed me... "Let's go back to bed..."

"Okay..." I sighed as we climbed back up on the bed and Bazil held me as we went to sleep...

Chapter 9

"Beautiee..." Bazil whispered as he kissed me awake...

"Mmmm... Yes my Thirst Quencher?"

"It's time to get ready..."

"Okay..." I breathed... "I'm ready..." I breathed again as I pulled him down on top of me and kissed him...

"Beautiee... we can't – the car will be downstairs waiting for us at 6:30..."

"Okay..." I said as I got up... "But you owe me..."

"You can collect anytime you want..." he breathed as he came up behind me and started nibbling on my ear...

"Stop it!" I laughed...

"Is that what you want?"

"Yes – otherwise I won't get dressed..."

"Okay..." he laughed... "I'll stop..." After we got dressed, I turned to look at Bazil... and I couldn't help myself...

"Beautiee..." he breathed as I kissed him so hard I startled him...

"You look so fucking good..." I breathed...

"You're gonna pay for that later..." he said as he smiled at me mischeviously...

"You promise?" Bazil didn't answer me. We went out into the hallway, got in the elevator, and went down to the lobby...

"Mr. & Mrs. Osgood — We've been expecting you — come with me..." the host said as we followed him into the nightclub and waited to be seated... "Our server will be with you in a few moments... Welcome to the Marquee..."

"I've always wanted to come here..." I gushed...

"I just wanna make you happy..." Bazil sighed...

"That's not true..."

"Beautiee!"

"You don't just wanna make me happy..." I said as I pulled him into a kiss... "You wanna love me..."

"Damn right I do..." Bazil said as he kissed me back...

"Good evening Mr. & Mrs. Osgood — my name is Winston — I'll be your server this evening — here's our menu — please let me know what you'd like..." he said as he handed the menu to Bazil...

"Hmmm... I'm not sure... Tuna Poke Tacos, Chile Relleno Empanadas, Grilled Cheese & Tomato Soup Dumplings, Avocado Lemon &

Espelette Toast, Beets an Creamy Burrata Toast
– Beautiee – what do you think?"

"Grilled Cheese & Tomato Soup
Dumplings…"

"Really?"

"Yea – I haven't had grilled cheese &
tomato soup since I was a kid…" I laughed…

"Very good…" Winston said… "Would you
like the Kale & Apple Salad or the House Salad?"

"Kale & Apple!" we both answered in
unison…

"Hmmm… Thai Style Deep-Fried Shrimp,
Oven Braised Chicken Meatballs, Spaghettini,
Grilled Atlantic Salmon… Beautiee – what would
you like?" Bazil asked…

"I'd like the Thai Shrimp and I want you to
get the Chicken Meatballs – this way we can
share…"

"Very good…" Winston said…

"Okay Beautiee – I think I know what we
want from this selection – Blistered Shishito
Peppers, Mediterranean Cauliflower, or BBQ
Fries…"

"BBQ Fries!" I laughed…

"Very good – your dessert will be Flourless
Chocolate Cake Pops – can I get you something to
drink?" Winston asked…

"Hmmm… what do you suggest?" Bazil
asked…

"You'll have your choice of a bottle later tonight – if you want to stay sober until then – I'd suggest ginger ale or Pepsi..." Winston laughed...

"Amaretto Sour!" We said in unison...

"Very good – I'll be back with your drinks..." Winston said as he left the table...

"Thank you Bazil..."

"You don't have to thank me Beautiee..."

"I know... but I'm going to..."

"Okay... thank you too..." Bazil laughed...

"Here's your drinks – your food will be out shortly..." Winston said as he placed our drinks on the table and walked away..."

"Here's to us..." Bazil said as he lifted his glass...

"To us..." I said as I raised my glass and we both took a sip...

"Excuse me..." she said as she hurried over to our table...

"Yes?" Bazil answered...

"I'm sorry – I don't mean to disturb you – but can we have a picture?"

"I'm with my wife..."

"Oh – Mrs. Osgood – I'm sorry – I meant no disrespect..."

"That's okay – Bazil you can take a picture with them if you want..."

"You sure?"

"Yea... I'm sure..."

"Okay ladies – let's make this quick – I wanna get back to my wife..."

"Okay!" they squealed as they sat beside him and took a few selfies...

"Mrs. Osgood – can we take a picture with you too?"

"Me?"

"Yeeaasss – I wanna be the first one to be in a picture with Bazil's wife!" she squealed as they both sat down beside me and took selfies...

"Oooh girl – they gonna be hatin!" her friend said...

"Okay ladies – I need my wife back..." Bazil laughed...

"Sorry – thank you!" they squealed as they hurried off...

"Ummm... Bazil?"

"Yes Beautiee?"

"You wanna tell me what just happened?"

"That happens a lot..."

"Why?"

"I'm somewhat of a celebrity..."

"Are you a record producer?"

"Huh – I wish..."

"Bazil... I..."

"You have nothing to worry about..." Bazil said as he pulled me into a kiss...

"You promise?"

"I promise..." Bazil might as well have told me I should be worried because I was...

"Here's your food – enjoy!" Winston said as he put our food down on the table... "Shall I get you another?" he asked as he picked up my glass...

"Yes please!" I answered...

"I'll also have another..." Bazil said. We started eating and I didn't speak. Bazil could tell I was pre-occupied... "Beautiee?"

"Yes Bazil?"

"You okay?"

"Yea..."

"You want some meatballs?"

"Sure... you want some shrimp?"

"Sure..." Bazil said as he reached in my plate, took some shrimp, and gave me some meatballs... "It's good...

"Yes... it is..."

"You sure you're okay?" Bazil asked as he took my hand and kissed it...

"Yes Bazil..." I said as I pulled him into a kiss... "I'm fine..."

"You're fine alright..." Bazil said as he started feeling my leg under the table...

"Bazil! Stop it!" I laughed...

"No..." Bazil whispered in my ear as he moved his hand up my thigh...

"Ready for dessert?" Winston asked as he came to the table...

"I am!" I answered...

"We're ready for dessert..." Bazil laughed...

"Very well – I'll be back..." Winston said as he went to get our dessert...

"You owe me..." Bazil whispered in my ear...

"I know..." I giggled...

"I'm going to collect..." he whispered... "and when I do..." he whispered as he kissed my neck... "no one will stop me..." he whispered as he moved his hand up my thigh, moved my panties to the side and inserted two fingers inside me...

"Bazil..."

"Ssshhh..." he whispered as Winston came back to the table with our dessert...

"Will there be anything else?" Winston asked as Bazil finger-fucked me slowly, torturing me...

"No... No thank you..." I stuttered...

"Nothing else for me..." Bazil said as he pulled his fingers out of me, put his arm around me, pulled me close to him, put his other hand under the table, moved up my thigh, moved my panties to the side, inserted two fingers inside me, and started fucking me again...

"Bazil..." I moaned...

"Yes Beautiee..." he breathed as he kissed me hard and massaged my G-spot...

"Bazil... Shit... I'm Cumming..."

"Cum for me..." Bazil breathed as he kissed me...

"Huh... Huh... Huh... Huh... Huh..." I moaned in Bazil's mouth as he continued massaging my G-spot and I had a few minigasms... "Mmmm..." he moaned in my mouth as he pulled his fingers out of me, picked up a chocolate cake pop, and alternated between licking the cake pop and his fingers...

"Mmm... these are really good!" I exclaimed as I bit into one of the cake pops...

"They certainly are..." he said as he smiled at me mischievously...

"I can't wait to collect what you owe me..."

"I'm looking forward to it..."

"The club will be opening soon - please come with me..." Winston said as we got up and followed him up to level 2 to our table in VIP and sat down... "Here's what you have to choose from..." Winston said as he handed Bazil the menu... "We also provide security for your comfort and safety..."

"I guess you saw what happened earlier..." Bazil laughed...

"Yes sir..."

"I didn't think I'd be recognized here..." Bazil laughed...

"Once you become a celebrity – you can't hide anywhere..."

"I guess not..." Bazil laughed as he looked at the menu... "Okay Beautiee – they have a lot to choose from... depending on what you want..."

"Are you on the menu?" I asked as I moved closer to him, put my arm around him, and started kissing him on his neck...

"Mmmm... that's nice..."

"I'll come back..." Winston said as he walked away...

"Beautiee..." Bazil laughed... "Stop..."

"No..." I breathed as I continued kissing him on his neck and started rubbing his dick...

"Beautiee... stop..."

"No..." I breathed as I straddled him and rubbed my clit on his dick...

"Beautiee... I'm warning you..." Bazil said before I kissed him hard...

"That's it!" Bazil said as he pushed me off his lap, jumped up, and ran down the corridor...

"Bazil! Are you okay?" I yelled as I ran after him...

"I gotta go!" he answered as he ran into the men's room. I waited outside a few minutes... and then I got worried...

"Bazil?" I called out as I peeked in the men's room... "Bazil? Are you sick?" I asked as I went into the men's room and closed the door...

"Gotcha!" he said as he came out the stall, rushed past me, and locked the door...

"Bazil! I thought you were sick!"

"I know..." he said as he pulled me into a kiss, held me close to him, went up under my dress, and ripped my panties off...

"Bazil..." I breathed...

"Didn't I tell you to stop?" he growled as he picked me up, put me on the sink, and pushed my legs open...

"Yeesss..." I breathed...

"What did you do?" he growled as he thrust himself inside me...

"I... I... Ooohhh... Bazil..."

"Now..." he growled as he started thrusting... "This is what happens when you don't listen..."

"Bazil... Fuck me..."

"Uggh! Uggh! Uggh! Uggh!"

"Aaagh! Aaagh! Aaagh! Aaagh! Aaaaagggghhhh!"

"Uuugh! Uuugh! Uuugh! Uuugh! Uuugggghhhh!"

"I'm gonna tell you no more often..." I breathed...

"Is that right?" he breathed...

"Hell yea..." I breathed as we started kissing...

"Anybody in here?" someone yelled...

"Just a sec..." Bazil said a she went over to the toilet, peed, and then came back over to the sink...

"I might as well pee too..." I whispered as I went over to the toilet, peed, flushed, and went over to the sink. We both washed our hands, dried them, and Bazil opened the door...

"Sorry about that..." he said as he walked out and I walked out behind him...

"Ohh... that's okay!" the man laughed as he went into the bathroom...

"I love you..." Bazil said as he pulled me into a kiss...

"I love you too..."

"C'mon – let's go get drunk..." Bazil laughed as we went back over to the VIP area.

Chapter 10

"There you are!" Winston said...

"Sorry about that – we needed to use the bathroom..." Bazil said...

"No apologies necessary – I'll go to another table while you look over the menu..." Winston said as he walked away...

"Are you on the menu?" I asked as I moved closer to Bazil and kissed him on his neck...

"Yes... if that's what you want..."

"Okay..." I sighed...

"If you want vodka they have Hangar One, Effen, and Absolut..."

"I don't want any vodka..."

"If you want tequila they have Cuervo Tradicional Blanco, El Tesoro Blanco, or Avion Silver..."

"I don't want any tequila either..."

"If you want rum they have Diplomatico Reserva Exclusiva – 12 year, Bacardi Silver, Mount Gay Eclipse, or Captain Morgan..."

"Hmmm... how about Bacardi Silver?"

"You want that instead of Captain Morgan?'

"I already have a Lil' Captain in me..." I breathed as I pulled him into a kiss...

"Are you ready?" Winston asked...

"Yes – we'll have a bottle of Bacardi Silver..." Bazil answered...

"You're newlyweds – right?"

"Yes..."

"Hmmm... ˗ I'm surprised you don't want champagne..."

"No thank you – champagne goes to my head way too fast..." I laughed. Bazil just looked at me and smiled mischievously...

"I'll be back with your Bacardi Silver..." Winston said as he went to get our bottle and they started to play Baby by Brandy...

"Dance with me..." I said as I pulled Bazil up and we started dancing...

"Here's your Bacardi – is there anything else you need?" Winston asked...

"Shot glasses!" I yelled over the music and then I started singing to Bazil... "Baby, Baby, Baby, Baby... Don't you know that you're so fine?"

"Yes I know..." Bazil laughed. Winston came back with the shot glasses, put them on the table, and walked away. Bazil stopped dancing, opened the bottle, poured us a shot, handed one to me, and we drank...

"Ohhh... Mr. Osgood... you're gonna get me drunk..." I laughed...

"I know..." he laughed...

"Ohhh... I love this song!" I said as I started dancing to Don't Disturb This Groove by The System. Bazil pulled me close to him, held me, and sang to me as we continued dancing...

"Pay attention, are you listening, you're my favorite girl..."

"I love you..."

"I love you too..." Bazil poured us another shot and we danced until In The Mood by Johnny Gill started playing. Bazil sat down, pulled me down beside him, and said... "This song reminds me of the night I first saw you..."

"Oh Bazil..." I sighed as I started crying...

"Uh uh uh..." he said as he kissed my tears and my mouth..."

"I can't help it... I cry when I'm happy..." Bazil poured us another shot and then What's It Feel Like by Montell Jordan started playing and we got up to dance...

"I know it feels good..." Bazil breathed in my ear..."

"Yeesss..." I breathed. We continued dancing and as soon as Don't Talk by Jon B came on, Bazil stopped to pour us another shot and then he repeated the lyrics verbatim...

"Don't talk, baby just roll with me, take a sip, kinda got you feeling dizzy, it's alright Baby if it's alright with you..."

"Yes..." I moaned... "It's alright..." We continued dancing until Bazil heard I'll Do 4 U by Father MC. He stopped to pour us a shot and we continued dancing until Bazil heard House Call by Shabba Ranks. Bazil stopped dancing, poured us another shot, pulled me close to him, and proceeded to tell me how my body couldn't lie to him as we danced...

"Your body can't lie to me... can it Beautiee?"

"No My Thirst Quencher..."

"'Cause I know just what you're needing... and I give you what you need... don't I?"

"Yes My Thirst Quencher..."

"Damn right I do..." he slurred as we continued dancing. Bazil stopped to pour us another shot as I'm So Into You by SWV came on... "Are you into me Beautiee?"

"Yes My Thirst Quencher..."

"You're so into me you don't know what you're gonna do..."

"I'm gonna love you..."

"I'm gonna love you too..." We continued dancing until No Diggity by Black Street started playing. Bazil poured us another shot and started talking shit to me... "You like the way I work it..."

"Yes My Thirst Quencher..." I laughed...

"What's so funny?"

"You like the way I work it too..." I laughed...

"Damn right I do..." Bazil said as he pulled me into a kiss. When That's The Way Love Goes by Janet Jackson came on, Bazil poured us another shot and continued talking shit... "You wanna take me there?"

"Yes My Thirst Quencher..."

"Do I make you feel so good you wanna cry?"

"Yes My Thirst Quencher... Yes..."

"You make me feel so good I wanna cry too..." he said and then he started crying...

"Bazil... please... don't cry..." I said as I kissed his eyes and his mouth..."

"I'm okay... I'm just happy... like you..." he said as he kissed me. We continued dancing until Too Close by Next came on and Bazil poured the last two shots for us... "Do you feel that Beautiee?"

"Yes My Thirst Quencher..."

"You do that..."

"Damn right I do!" I laughed. We continued dry fucking until Party Ain't A Party by Queen Pen started playing and then we went back to dancing until the song was over...

"I'm drunk!" Bazil laughed...

"So am I..." I laughed...

"I gotta go..."

"You sick again?" I laughed...

"No..." he laughed... 'I really gotta go..."

"I gotta go too..."

"C'mon – let's go…" Bazil laughed as we started down the corridor…

"The ladies room is right here…" security said…

"Okay – I'll be right out…" I laughed as I went in, used the toilet, washed my hands, and came out…

"That was fast…" Bazil laughed…

"It was a straight shot!" I laughed as security watched us stumble down the corridor to the men's room…

"Wait here _ I'll be right back…"

"Okay…" I said as he went into the men's room and I took off my shoes…

"Where are your shoes?" he asked as he came out the bathroom…

"In my hand…"

"Why aren't they on your feet?" he laughed…

"'Cause I'm drunk…" I laughed…

"Okay… let's go home…" he said as he pulled me close to him and we stumbled down the corridor past the VIP section to the stairs…

"You go ahead – I'll come down after you…"

"Beautiee – I'm fine…"

"I know you're fine… but I'm not…" I laughed…

"Okay…" he said as he went downstairs. Bazil watched as I took my time walking down the stairs. When I got to the bottom he picked me up… "You're okay too…" he said as he pulled me into a kiss…

"Yes… I am…" I breathed…

"You ready to go home?"

"Yes…"

"Okay – c'mon…" he said as he put his arm around me and we went outside…

"Mr. & Mrs. Osgood – right this way…" the driver said as he escorted us to our limousine…

"Oh shit – that's Bazil Osgood!" I heard somebody say…

"Who the fuck is she?" I heard somebody ask…

"Girl – shut the fuck up - didn't you just hear the man say Mr. & Mrs. Osgood?"

"Oh shit! I didn't know he was married!"

"Well now you know…" I said loud enough for her to hear me as I looked her in her face to make sure she understood me…

"Oh shit! You lucky she ain't bust yo' ass… C'mon!" I heard somebody say as we got in the limousine…

"Driver – can you put this up?" I asked…

"Yes Maam…" the driver answered as he put up the privacy window…

"Beautiee… what… Ooohhh…" he moaned as I took his dick in my mouth…

"Mine…" I breathed as I took his dick out my mouth… and then put it back in…

"Yes… yours…" he moaned as he pushed my head down on his dick until he was hitting the back of my throat... and then I took his dick out my mouth and sat up... "Beautiee... what the..."

"Gotcha!" I said and then I bust out laughing...

"Ohh... okay..." he said as he put his dick back in his pants. Bazil was quiet the rest of the ride back to the hotel. When the driver opened the door, Bazil got out, helped me out, and we went back into the hotel, through the lobby, and into the elevator. Bazil didn't say anything and I was worried. When we got off the elevator Bazil took my hand as we walked to our room...

"We didn't take any pictures..." I said as we went inside and Bazil closed the door...

"Don't worry..." he said as he pulled me into a kiss... "You can go to the website, click on tonight, and you can download as many pictures as you want..."

"Mmm..." I thought you were mad at me...

"I don't get mad..." he said as he started to undress me... "but I do get even..."

"You started it..." I laughed as he tickled me...

"I started it..." he breathed as he kissed me... "and now... I'm going to finish it..." he breathed as he pushed me down on the bed...

"I'm drunk..." I laughed as I hit the bed...

"Are you okay?" he asked as he started taking off his clothes...

"I'm dizzy..."

"Yea... you're drunk..." he laughed as he got on the bed and lay down beside me...

"I feel like I'm gonna fall off the bed..." I laughed...

"You ever have drunk sex?" I bust out laughing...

"What's so funny?"

"I don't remember!"

"I'm going to change that..." he breathed as he kissed me...

"You're not drunk?"

"Yes... I'm drunk..." he laughed...

"How..."

"I'm used to it..." he said as he got up on his knees...

"What are you doing?' I breathed...

"What's it feel like I'm doing?" he asked as he picked up my foot and started kissing me from my ankle and continued kissing me up to my knee...

"Ooohhh... I like that..."

"Does it feel good?" he asked as he kissed his way up to my thigh..."

"Yes... it feels good..."

"Mmmm..." he moaned as he started sucking my thigh...

"Ooohhh..."

"Would you like me to suck anything else?" he asked as he smiled at me mischievously...

"Yes... please..." I breathed...

"Okay... I'll start here..." he breathed as he took my right nipple in his mouth and sucked it...

"Ooohhh..."

"Mmmm... you like that..."

"Yes... I like that..."

"Okay... I'll move over here..." he breathed as he took my left nipple in his mouth and sucked it...

"Ooohhh..."

"Mmmm... you like that too..."

"Yes... I like that too..."

"Hmmm... I have an idea..." he breathed as he started kissing me down my stomach...

"Yeesss...." I moaned...

"Mmmm... you already feel my lips on your pussy don't you?"

"Yes... Ooohhh... Bazil!" I moaned as he started sucking my clit hard... "Haah... Haah... Haah..."

"Mmmm... Yes Beautiee... Feed me..." he growled as he picked me up by my ass and went back to licking, sucking and slurping...

"Haah... Haah... Haah... Bazil... I'm cumming! I'm cumming! I'm cumming!" Bazil continued licking, sucking, and slurping as I continued having minigasms... and then he stuck his tongue inside me and started sucking again... "Bazil! Haah... Haah..."

"Mmmm...." He moaned as he licked, sucked, and slurped until my legs stopped shaking... "Now..." he breathed as he put me back down on the bed, lay on top of me, and kissed me.... "What would you like to do next?"

"I wanna finish what I started..." I breathed...

"I'd like that..." Bazil breathed as he got up off me and lay down on his back...

"Woah..." I laughed... "I'm still dizzy..." I laughed as I tried to get up...

"Easy Beautiee... not so fast..."

"Okay..." I breathed as I got down between his legs and took his dick in my mouth...

"Beautiee..." he moaned...

"I'm so drunk..." I laughed with his dick in my mouth...

"I can tell..." Bazil laughed. I closed my eyes, pictured his dick in my mind, and went back to sucking... "Beautiee... Ooohhh... Shit... Fuck... I'm cumming! Uuuggghhhh! Beautiee..." he called as he smoothed my hair away from my face... "Beautiee..." he called again... and then he bust out laughing when he realized I passed out with his dick in my mouth.

Chapter 11

"Oh God... my head..." I moaned...

"Good morning..." Bazil whispered as he kissed me...

"Good morning..." I breathed...

"I made coffee..."

"Ohhh... that sounds..." I started to say as I jumped up outta bed and ran to the bathroom... "Uuuggghh!" I groaned as I hurled up whatever I had left from last night into the toilet...

"Are you okay?" Bazil asked as he came into the bathroom...

"I'm sorry..." I sighed...

"For what?"

"I'm sorry you have to see me like this..." I sighed...

"Beautiee..." he said as he came over to me, pulled me to him, and kissed me...

"Yes Bazil?"

"Don't ever apologize to me for the way you look – understand?"

"Yes Bazil..." I sighed...

"I want you to take this cloth, pat your face, and come with me... you need coffee..."

"I need some mouthwash..."

"That's the last thing you need..."

"I just threw up..."

"And if you use mouthwash and try to drink a cup of coffee you'll be throwing up again..." he said as he pulled me to him and kissed me again...

"How can you kiss me after I just threw up?" I asked...

"Hmmm... let me see... nothing in your hair... nothing on your face... nothing on your lips... oh wait... I see something... let me get that cloth..." he said as he got the cloth and wiped my eyes... "There..." he said as he kissed me again...

"I love you..."

"I love you too – c'mon – you need to hurry up and start drinking..." he said as he put his arm around me and walked me into the dining room...

"No... please... no more... I can't..."

"Beautiee... here..." he said as he handed me two Tylenol capsules...

"What's this for?"

"Your headache..." I took the capsules from him and swallowed them...

"Oh no – you need to drink something..."

"I am going to drink something – I'm drinking coffee..."

"Here..." he said as he put a small glass of water in front of me. I took a few sips of water and put the glass back down on the table...

"I don't want anymore..."

"Okay – I'll get us some coffee..." he said as he went over to the coffee station, made us both coffee, came back to the table, sat down, and put the cups of coffee on the table. Bazil watched as I picked up my coffee and sipped it cautiously...

"Ooohhh... this is soo good!" I exclaimed...

"So... how much do you remember from last night?"

"Well..." I said as I started thinking about last night and smiled... "I think I remember everything..."

"You do?"

"I think so..." I answered as we continued drinking our coffee...

"Tell me..."

"We went to the Beauty & Essex Marquee Nightclub...

"Yes... we did..."

"You looked so good... I kissed you..."

"You did..."

"You told me you were going to make me pay for that..."

"So far so good... but you weren't drunk yet..."

"You looked at the menu – our server's name was Winston..."

"Okay..."

"We had Amaretto Sours..."

"We did..."

"Those ladies came to take a picture with you..."

"You didn't like that..."

"It's fine – it was unexpected – but when you told them you were with your wife they apologized – and then they wanted to be the first ones to take a picture with Ms. Osgood..."

"That's right... I still don't think you were drunk though..."

"I wasn't drunk – but I was feeling those drinks we had before we got our bottle..."

"I know..."

"You fucked me at the table... and I came all over your fingers..."

"Yess..."

"We went to our table in the VIP section... I asked you if you were on the menu... I started kissing your neck... I started rubbing your dick... I sat on your lap... and I started rubbing my clit on your dick..."

"Were you gonna cum?"

"Were you?"

"Maybe..."

"You warned me to stop... I didn't listen... so you tricked me by pretending you were sick so you could get me to come into the men's room... and it worked..."

"Yeess... it did..."

"You ripped my panties off... you picked me up... you put me on the sink... and you fucked me..."

"I did..." he said as he started rubbing his chin...

114

"Somebody was waiting to use the men's room..." I laughed...

"That's right..."

"You said let's go get drunk..."

"I did..."

"We started dancing... we got the bottle... you opened it... we drank shots..."

"We did..."

"I cried... you cried..."

"Yes..."

"I sang to you... you sang to me... and you talked a lot of shit!" I laughed...

"I wasn't talking shit..." he laughed... "I was telling it like it is..."

"We were so drunk!" I laughed...

"We were..."

"When we got outside, I heard somebody say that's Bazil Osgood..."

"You did?"

"Yes... and I also heard somebody ask who the fuck is she?"

"Where was I?"

"You were in the limousine already..."

"I'm sorry..."

"I heard somebody say shut the fuck up didn't you just hear the man say Mr. & Mrs. Osgood? And somebody else said I didn't know he was married... and I got up in her face and said well now you know..."

"I'm really sorry..."

"I pulled your dick out and sucked it..."

"Yeesss..."

"I thought you got mad 'cause I stopped and said gotcha..." I laughed...

"I wasn't mad..."

"When we got back in the room, you told me you don't get mad... you get even..."

"That's right..."

"I told you you started it..."

"And I told you I was going to finish it..."

"And then you finished it..." I sighed...

"Oh so you remember that?"

"Oh God... Yeesss..."

"Did you enjoy it?"

"I was on 100!" I laughed...

"Your legs were shaking..."

"I wanna do it again..." I sighed...

"We can do that..."

"I remember I tried to get up so I could suck your dick... and I got dizzy..." I laughed...

"You did..."

"I know I sucked your dick... but I don't remember anything after that..."

"That's because you passed out with my dick in your mouth!" he laughed...

"I did?"

"You did..."

"So you didn't get to cum?"

"I did..."

"Oh... okay..." I sighed...

"I wanna take you home..."

"Okay..."

"Are you sure?"

"Yea..."

"We can stay another day or two if you want..."

"I wanna go home... but I still have a hangover..."

"Okay – how 'bout we spend the rest of the day in bed – and then we check out and go home tomorrow afternoon?"

"Okay..." I yawned...

"I'll be right back..." he said as he got up and went to order room service...

"Good morning... yes we'd like coffee... yes we'll have the same order as before... okay... thank you..." he said as he hung up and came back to sit at the table with me...

"Do we have any coffee left?"

"No..."

"Oh okay..." I sighed as I got up, went over to him, straddled him, sat on his dick, and started riding as he held me...

"Ohhh... Beautiee..."

"Yeess..." I moaned...

"I remember this too..."

"So do I..."

"I... Ohhh..."

"Shit..."

"I'm gonna cum..."

"Go ahead..."

"Cum with me..."

"Is that what you want?"

"Oh God... Yes... I'm cumming!"

"Uuugh!   Uuugh!   Uuugh!   Uuugh! Uuuuggghhh!"

"I can't wait to go back to bed..." I breathed...

"Neither can I..." he breathed as I got up...

"Where are you going?"

"I'm going to get my cell phone..." I said as I went into the bedroom. When I came back to the table and sat down, Bazil looked confused...

"You need to make a call? Now?"

"Nooo..." I laughed...

"Okay..."

"I'm going to look at the pictures from the Marquee..."

"Oh... okay..."

"Ooohhh look!" I squealed. Bazil came and sat beside me to look at the picture...

"Oh that's nice..."

"I like it – I'm doing to download it..."

"You're going to download a picture of me with two other women?"

"Yes..."

"Why?"

"Why not?" I laughed... "Oh – look at this one!" I squealed...

"Oh that's really nice!"

"I'm downloading this one too!"

"I wonder where they posted it."

"Oh who knows – probably Instagram... Oooohhh.... Bazil... Look!"

"Oh wow…"

"It looks like I'm fucking you right there!" I laughed as I downloaded it…

"And that's exactly what everyone will think we were doing…" Bazil laughed…

"I don't give a fuck what they think!" I laughed as room service knocked on the door…

"Just a sec…" Bazil said as he got up to open the door…

"Good morning – shall I bring this in for you?"

"No thank you…"

"Okay – have a good day…"

"Breakfast is here… and so is coffee…" Bazil said as he poured us more coffee, added creamer, added sugar, and passed my cup to me…

"Thank you…" I breathed as I started drinking…

"You're welcome… How are you feeling?" he asked as we started eating…

"I'm starting to feel better…"

"I shouldn't've given you so much to drink…"

"I knew what I was doing…"

"You certainly did…"

"You're thinking about me sucking your dick – aren't you?"

"Yeesss…."

"You want more?"

"Yeesss… please…"

"Okay…" I said as we finished eating… "Let's go back to bed… and I'll give you more…" I said as we got up from the table and went back into the bedroom….

"Good morning…" I said as I answered the phone…

"Good morning Mrs. Osgood – this is Ms. DeNino…"

"Hi Roselle!" I squealed…

"I'm calling to let you know your video and pictures are ready…"

"Honey – the video and pictures are ready…"

"You wanna go pick them up?" Bazil asked…

"No…"

"You sure?"

"Yes…"

"Okay – I'll send them to you – it'll take a few days – is that alright?" Roselle asked…

"That's fine…" I sighed…

"Okay – congragulations…"

"Thank you…" I said as I hung up, sat on the bed, and pulled Bazil in front of me…

"Good morning!" I laughed…

"Good morning Mrs. Osgood – is everything okay?"

"Everything's fine…" I laughed…

"That's good – this is Melanie from the Spa…"

"Hi Melanie…"

"I was calling to see if you'd be interested in purchasing any of the items we used from your treatment yesterday..."

"Oh wow – my husband and I were talking about that..."

"You were?"

"Yes – we'd like to purchase everything..."

"Everything?"

"Everything – and Melanie?"

"Yes Mrs. Osgood?"

"Will the items come with instructions?"

"Absolutely..."

"Good..."

"Okay! Would you like to come pick up the items now?" she asked as Bazil untied his robe and stood in front of me...

"Ummm... no..." I stuttered... "We're checking out tomorrow – can you package them and we pick them up at the front desk?"

"Sure... I can do that..."

"Thank you..."

"Mrs. Osgood?"

"Yes Melanie?" I answered as Bazil started stroking his dick in front of me...

"Shall I charge it to the card we have on file?"

"Mmmm Hmmm..." I answered as I leaned over and took Bazil's dick in my mouth...

"Okay – everything will be packaged and left at the front desk for you in time for check out..." she said as Bazil took the phone from me, placed it in the cradle, took my head with both hands, and pushed his dick in further.

Chapter 12

"Welcome home Mrs. Osgood..." Bazil said as he picked me up in his arms, opened the door, and carried me inside...

"Ooohhh... I love it!" I said as I wrapped my arms around his neck and kissed him...

"Make yourself at home..." he said as he put me down... "I'm going to go back out to the car to get our bags..."

"Okay!" I squealed as he went outside... "I don't know where to go first – what's this room here?" I asked out loud as I opened the door and went inside... "Oooohhh... a library! My books will look great on that shelf!" I said as Bazil came in...

"I see you've found the library..."

"Yessss..."

"You like it?"

"I love it! I can't wait to come in here and write books..."

"You write books?"

"Yea..."

"I'm a publisher..." he said as he smiled...

"Oh my God! What kind of books do you publish? Where's your publishing company? How long have you been a publisher?"

"I started Osgood Publishing when I was 20 years old. At that time, I had five books published. I applied for business capital and used that capital to purchase the location in Milford, Connecticut. I was the only employee in that building at the time – but I didn't worry about how I was going to make enough money to cover the overhead – I did what I do – I wrote more books – sometimes I had nothing left after the bills were covered – but I never let that discourage me – I thanked God I had fans that supported me – and then something happened..."

"What happened?"

"I was in the office and my phone rang. I answered it and the caller identified himself as Samuel Logan. Sam asked me if I was hiring..." Bazil answered...

"And were you hiring?"

"No..."

"Oh wow..."

"But I asked him to come in for an interview..."

"Wait a minute – you weren't hiring – and you asked him to come in for an interview?"

"Yes..."

"Once Sam got there, he saw I was the only employee in the building and I thought he was going to leave – but instead – he sat down, he showed me his resume, and he told me if I gave him a chance he'd help me grow my company – so I hired him as my Vice President & CEO..."

"Okay – wait a minute – you just said you barely had any money after you paid your bills – and you gave him the job as Vice President & CEO?"

"Yes..."

"Okay – you gave him the job – what happened after that?"

"Sam hit the ground running – he hired his wife as his Personal Assistant – and he hired his mother-in-law as our Chief Financial Officer..."

"Okay – wait – what?"

"When he saw that I was the only employee and he didn't turn around and run... I knew..."

"Aww..."

"The first thing Sam did was apply for more capital so we could purchase printing equipment, press machines, etc. – I was outsourcing these and Sam showed me how I could do everything in-house – and reduce my expenses..."

"So you started making money right away..."

"Basically ‐ that's when we hired Joselyn – and then we hired Sheila..."

"Aww..."

"So tell me about your publishing company..."

"I've always been a writer. I grew up in foster care and writing was how I dealt with it..."

"You grew up in foster care?"

"Yea..."

"I'm sorry..." Bazil said as he pulled me into a hug and I continued... "As a child, I would write songs, poems, and essays. When it was time for me to graduate from elementary shool, the Principal asked us to write an essay about our experiences and I wrote an essay about the way they teased me when I had eye surgery and had to wear prisms on my glasses – I even wrote a song about it to help me cope..."

"You've been through a lot..." he said as he kissed me...

"Yea... I have..." I sighed and then I continued... "I was surprised when the principal told me my essay was chosen to be read at the Graduation Assembly and I sang the song I wrote to the Assembly..."

"You sang... about how you were teased... to the Graduation Assembly? How'd that go?"

"It was actually funny..."

"Funny? How so?"

"They were laughing with me instead of laughing at me..."

"Aww..."

"As I got older, I would read books, critique them, and change the ending by saying I would have said this, I would have done that. My friends would always tell me you should write a book and I would always say one day – and one day finally came. I published my 1st book with a vanity publisher in 2003, I made mistakes, and I learned what I didn't like about vanity publishers. Since writing is in my blood, rather than give up on publishing, I went to writing expos, author signings, etc., and learned some more. The turning point for me was when I had a one-on-one with Michael Baisden who sat with me, gave me advice, and took out his tape recorder to make a note when he thought I had a good idea!"

"Michael Baisden was a mentor to you?"

"Yes he was…"

"Awww…"

"After I met with him I started from scratch - I turned my first book into a 5-book series, and I was ready to publish them but I knew I wasn't going back to vanity publishing so I reached out to David L. at Total Package Publications…."

"Where'd you meet him?"

"I met him in Facebook at first, and then he started hosting Author Meet-N-Greets and I met him in person…"

"Oh wow…"

"He referred me to selfpublishing.com, and they gave me step-by-step instructions on the entire process from purchasing your own ISBN numbers to starting your own publishing company, so I started Beautiful Publications in 2014 and published my series myself..."

"Oh so you have an LLC?"

"Yea..."

"So..." he said as he pulled me to him and held me... "What kind of books do you publish?"

"Erotic Fiction..."

"You like erotica?"

"Yes..."

"Why Erotica?" he asked as he kissed me on my neck...

"Because..." I breathed as he pulled me into a kiss... "I love writing... and..." I started to say but I was interrupted by another kiss... "I love sex..."

"Mmmm... me too..."

"So far, I've only published my own books..."

"Oh so you haven't published any other authors?"

"Not yet..."

"Hmmm... interesting..."

"I wanna see the rest of the house..."

"Okay..." Bazil said as he took my hand and escorted me into the living room... "This is the living room..."

"Let's sit on the couch..." I said as I sat down...

"Is it comfortable?" he asked as he sat down beside me...

"I'm not sure yet..." I said as I pulled him down on top of me...

"Do you need us to test it?" he breathed as he kissed me...

"Not yet... I wanna see the rest of the house..."

"Okay..." he said as he got up and helped me up off the couch... "C'mon – I'll show you the kitchen..." he said as he took my hand and led me into the kitchen...

"Ooohhh... I love this kitchen!" I squealed as I walked around the island... "I wanted this in my kitchen..." I sighed...

"You have a house?"

"Yes..."

"In Connecticut?"

"In Bridgeport..."

"How many bedrooms?"

"Three..."

"We need to get your things..."

"Oh my God – you have a pool?"

"Yes..." he answered as he followed me outside...

"I wanna make love in the pool..."

"We can do that..." he said as he came up behind me and pulled me into his arms...

"Let's go upstairs – I wanna see our bedroom..."

"We have a suite..." he said as he took me by the hand, led me back inside, pulled me out the kitchen to the foyer, and started pulling me upstairs...

"Wait..." I laughed...

"I'm sorry..." he laughed... "I'm excited..."

"Me too..." I laughed as we both hurried upstairs... "Let's go this way!" I squealed as I went to the last room at the end of the hall... "Ohhh – you have laundry upstairs – nice!"

"I'm glad you like it..."

"And this must be a guest room..." I said as I went into the room... "Oh this is nice – I love the colors – we don't even need to change the colors – it works for a girl or a boy..."

"You see this room as a nursery?"

"Yea..." I sighed...

"You ready to see the master?"

"Yea..."

"Come with me..." he said as he took my hand and led me to the master bedroom...

"Oh my God!" I squealed as I ran to the king-sized bed and jumped on it...

"Is it comfortable?" he asked as he joined me on the bed, pulled me to him, and started kissing me...

"Yeesss..." I breathed...

"I can't wait to make love to you..."

"Neither can I – oh shoot – you have neighbors?' I asked as I jumped up to look out the window...

"Yea – my best friend, Troy – and his wife Keisha..."

"They can look right in here!"

"You don't have to worry about that..." he laughed...

"Maybe I don't have to worry about that – but I do have to worry about something else..."

"What's that?" he asked as he came up behind me..."

"The way you fuck me – they're going to hear a lot of moaning... and screaming..."

"I can close the window..." he laughed...

"Okay..."

"Let me show you the bathroom..." he said as he took me by the hand and led me to the bathroom...

"Oh Bazil!" I whispered with tears in my eyes...

"You don't like it?"

"I love it – two sinks – a luxurious tub – and a walk-in shower for two... with a bench..." I said as I looked at him mischievously...

"You wanna take a shower?"

"Yes... but can we do something first?"

"We can do whatever you want..." he said as he pulled me into a kiss...

"Can we go to my house?"

"In Bridgeport?"

"Sure... if that's what you want..."

"Okay!" I squealed as I turned and ran down the stairs...

"Beautiee – wait for me!" he laughed as he ran down the steps behind me...

Chapter 13

"This is cute..." he said as we pulled into the driveway...

"Thank you..." I said as I opened the door and jumped out the car...

"I guess you're excited..." he laughed...

"C'mon – I can't wait to show you!" I squealed as I got my keys out and opened the door...

"This is nice..." he said as he came inside... "How do you get upstairs?"

"The stairs are over there..." I answered as I pointed to the right...

"Hmmm... okay..."

"This is my office..." I said as I took his hand and led him into my office. Bazil didn't say anything. I watched him intently as he looked at the covers on the wall, my degree, awards, etc. and I was happy when he started smiling...

"Where are your books?"

"They're in the library..." I answered as I took his hand and led him into the library. Bazil looked around the library before he went over to the book case...

"How many books are in your series?"

"Five..."

"Okay..." he said as he opened the book case and took out two coffee mugs with my company logo and one of each book in the series...

"C'mon - I'll show you the rest of the house – this is the bathroom..."

"Okay..."

"This is the kitchen..."

"Hmmm... a galley kitchen..."

"This is the dining room..."

"It's a nice size for a small house..."

"This is the backyard..." I said as I opened the sliding doors and went out on the deck...

"This is nice – do you ever grill out here?"

"Yea – the grill sits here – I have a swing I put over there – let me show you the garage..." I said as I used the button on my keychain to open the garage door...

"This is a nice garage..."

"Now I'll take you down into the crawl space..." I said as I opened the door...

"Crawl space?"

"Yea – c'mon..." I said as we headed downstairs...

"So this is where you do laundry?"

"Yea..."

"And you have to carry it upstairs?"

"Yea..."

"Let's go upstairs..."

"Okay..." I said as I followed him up the stairs, into the kitchen, into the living room, and up the stairs...

"What's this?" he asked as he pointed to the doors....

"Storage..."

"May I?"

"Sure..."

"Hmmm... okay..." he said as he opened the doors, looked at the clothes, and closed the doors. We continued up the stairs until we reached the top of the stairs... "Wardrobe?"

"Yea..." Bazil opened the wardrobe, looked at himself in the mirror, and closed it...

"You don't need to look in the mirror – you look good..." I laughed...

"Oh yea?" he asked as he took me in his arms and started walking me backwards until we bumped into the dresser... "Is this another closet?"

"That's the bathroom..."

"It's small – but it's okay..." he said as he looked around in the bathroom...

"I wanted to dormer out and turn that into a walk-in shower for two..."

"Why didn't you?"

"I'm scared of renovations – everytime the contractor starts work they find something else that needs to be fixed..."

"How old is this house?"

"72 years old..."

"You should do it..."

"I don't need to..."

"Why not?"

"My husband already has a master suite..."

"Is that right?" he asked as he came out the bathroom, pulled me to him, and kissed me...

"Mmmm hmmm..." I moaned in his mouth...

"This is cozy..." he said as he started walking me backwards towards the bed...

"I like it..."

"Me too..." he said as he pushed me back on the bed and climbed on top of me...

"My bed isn't as comfortable as yours..." I breathed as he kissed me...

"I wonder..." he said as he kissed me and put my arms above my head... "What we have... in here!" he said as he snatched the drawer open to my nightstand...

"Bazil! Don't go in there!"

"Something you don't want me to see?" he asked as he held my arms above my head with one hand and felt around in the drawer with the other... until he found what he was looking for... and pulled my dildo out the drawer... "Hmmm... it's my complexion... but it's no match for me..." he said as he kissed me again...

"Mmmm mmm..." I moaned in his mouth. Bazil let go of my arms and began unbuttoning my blouse as he continued kissing me. He slid his hand up my body, removed my breasts from my bra, and alternated between licking them and sucking them...

"Bazil..." I moaned. Bazil kissed his way down my belly, unzipped my jeans, and pulled them down off of me along with my panties. He got on his knees, pulled his shirt over his head, tossed it in the chair, and looked down at me. He loosened his belt, slid his jeans and boxers off his ass, kicked them onto the floor, spread my legs, laid down on top of me... and put his tongue in my mouth as he ease himself inside me and started thrusting...

"Mmmmm... Mmmmm... Mmmmm... Mmmm..."

"Mmmph! Mmmph! Mmmph! Mmmph!" I grabbed Bazil's ass and squeezed it as I bent my legs and rocked on his dick...

"Hmmmm! Hmmmm! Hmmmm! Hmmmm!" Bazil grabbed my knees, spread my legs wider, and fucked me harder...

"Mmmph! Mmmph! Mmmph! Mmmph! My legs started trembling around him and he knew I was cumming...

"HMMMPH! HMMMPH! HMMPH! HMMPH!

"MMMPH! MMMPH! MMMPH! MMMPH!" Bazil turned me on my side and we continued kissing as our orgasms subsided...

"Let's go home..." I breathed...

"Let's go home..." he breathed as he kissed me again...

When we got home I couldn't get in the door fast enough. I ran upstairs... and Bazil closed the door, and ran upstairs behind me. I ran into the bedroom and stood there waiting. Bazil came into the bedroom, pulled me close to him, and kissed me as we started undressing each other. We continued kissing until we were both naked, and then he led me to the bed. I got up on the bed, spread my legs, and held my arms open, inviting Bazil to come to me, and he was happy to accept my invitation...

"So..." he whispered in my ear... "Are you hungry?"

"Yesss..." I moaned as he started kissing me on my neck...

"Are you hungry for food..." he breathed as he kissed me... "Or... are you hungry... for me?" he breathed as eased himself inside me...

"Both..." I moaned as he started thrusting...

"Beautiee..." he moaned...

"Bazil... Ooohhhh..."

"Uggh! Uggh! Uggh! Uggh!"

"Huh! Huh! Huh! Huh!"

"Is this what you want?" he asked as he fucked me harder and deeper...

"Oh Bazil... Yes... Fuck me..."

"Uggh! Uggh! Uggh! Uggh!"

"Bazil... Fuck me... I'm cumming..."

"I'm cumming with you...Uggh!"

"Aaagh! Aaagh! Aaagh! Aaagh!"

"Uuugh! Uuugh! Uuugh! Uuugh!"

"Damn that was good..." I breathed...

"Yes... it... was..." Bazil said between kisses...

"I'm really hungry Bazil..."

"Okay... I'll get up and make you something to eat..." he said between kisses...

"Okay..." I breathed...

"Let me up..." he laughed...

"I don't want to..."

"Mmmm.... I don't want you to either... but... if you don't let me up... I can't feed you..."

"Mmmm... okay..." I sighed as Bazil got up, put his robe on, and went downstairs. I got up, put on one of his robes, and went downstairs to the kitchen...

"What do you want?"

"You..." I sighed...

"What do you want to eat?"

"You..." I laughed...

"Hmmm... let me see what we have in here..." he said as he looked in the refrigerator... "Okay – I have bologna, ham, turkey, and cheese..."

"You need to go shopping..." I laughed...

"You're right – I do..." he laughed...

"You have Swiss cheese?"

"I have Swiss and American..."

"Okay – I'll have a sandwich..."

"Okay – you want bologna, ham, or turkey?"

"All of them..."

"Okay! You want Swiss or American?"

"Both..."

"Okay!   You want mayonnaise or mustard?"

"Mayonnaise..." I answered as he started laughing...

"What's so funny?"

"I thought you were gonna say both..." he laughed...

"You have anything in there to drink?"

"I got ginger ale and Pepsi..."

"I'll have Pepsi... in a glass... with a shot of Henny..."

"Okay! I'll have that too!" he said as he went to the library, got the bottle of Hennessey, and brought it back into the kitchen. I watched as he made our sandwiches, brought them to the table, and then he went back over to the counter to make our drinks...

"Your phone's ringing..."

"Oh shoot..." he said as he put the drinks down and sat down at the table...

"Aren't you gonna answer it?"

"I'll call them back..." he said as he picked up his sandwich and took a bite..."

"Okay..." I sighed as I picked up my sandwich and took a bite... "Oh my God..." this is sooo good... thank you..."

"You're welcome..."

"I can't wait to go to work with you..." I said as we ate...

"I can't wait to introduce you..."

"I hope everyone likes me..."

"They'll love you..."

"I'm nice... but I can be nasty if I need to be..."

"Were you ever a supervisor?"

"Yes..."

"Did you ever have to get nasty?"

"I went overboard once... I was really out of line..."

"Really?"

"Yea... I apologized to him the next day though..."

"I'm sure he appreciated it..."

"He said it was okay but I told him it wasn't okay because I wouldn't like it if it were done to me so I shouldn't do it to anyone else..."

"Yea... they'll love you..."

"You really think so?"

"It doesn't matter... "

"Why not?"

"Because..." he said as he leaned over and kissed me... "I love you..."

"I love you too..."

"To my beautiful wife..." he said as he picked up his glass..."

"To my beautiful husband..." I said as I picked up my glass and we both started drinking...

"Oh damn – I think I put too much Hennessey in here..." he laughed...

"Ohhh... this is good..." I moaned as I continued drinking and Bazil picked up his cell phone...

"Oh shit!" Bazil said as he read the text...

"What's wrong?"

"I gotta go..." Bazil said as he finished his drink and got up from the table...

"Bazil – what's wrong?"

"I'm sorry Beautiee – it's Trevor..." he said as he headed upstairs to get dressed...

"Your best friend? Is he alright?"

"He'll be okay – but I gotta go – I'll see you soon as I can..." he said as he pulled me into a kiss and hurried out the door...

Chapter 14

"Bazil..." Trevor exclaimed as he opened the door...

"Trevor..." Bazil breathed as he entered Trevor's apartment and closed the door...

"I missed you, Trevor breathed as he pulled Bazil into a deep, passionate kiss...

"I missed you too," Bazil said as he ran his hands down Trevor's back and grabbed his ass... "Did you give this sweet ass away while I was on my honeymoon?" Bazil asked as they embraced...

"No Baby..." Trevor breathed as he pulled Bazil back into another kiss...

"MmmmMmmm.... Good...." Bazil moaned as he backed Trevor towards the bedroom and they began undressing each other... "Le'me see that ass..." Bazil breathed as he pushed Trevor towards the bed and pushed him down on his back...

"Ooohhh... yes Daddy," Trevor moaned as Bazil climbed on top of Trevor and began kissing him and caressing him...

"Spread those legs for me..." Bazil moaned as he slipped on a condom and gently eased himself inside of Trevor...

"Damn I missed your dick," Trevor moaned...

"And I missed your sweet ass..." Bazil moaned as he began stroking Trevor...

"Yes Daddy... Fuck me... that's it... right there..." Trevor moaned...

"Mmmmmm..... You feel so good... ssshhhiiiiitttt..." Bazil moaned

"You about to make me cum Daddy..." Trevor moaned...

"Not yet Baby..." Bazil breathed... "It's been a while... I want to enjoy you," Bazil said as he slowed down and started kissing Trevor on his lips and on his neck...

"Oooohhhh... that feels good... feels like you missed me..."

"You have no idea Baby..." Bazil moaned as he began licking and sucking on Trevor's nipples...

"Oooohhh.... Oooohhh.... Oooohhhh..." Trevor moaned...

"Not yet baby... hold it for me..." Bazil moaned as he pulled out of Trevor's ass and moved down Trevor's belly, kissing him as he went...

"Oh Daddy..." Trevor moaned...

"Yes Baby..." Bazil moaned as he took Trevor's dick in his mouth...

"Daddy... Daddy... Daddy..." Trevor moaned as Bazil sucked his dick slowly, sensuously, and deliberately... "I can't hold it Daddy... I'm cccuuuummmmmiiiinnnngggg!" he screamed as Bazil stuck two fingers in Trevor's ass, massaging every last drop of Trevor's love nut from his balls, into his dick, and down into Bazil's throat... "Damn Daddy... you should get pussy more often it it's gonna make you miss me like this..." Trevor breathed while kissing Bazil...

"Indeed..." Bazil breathed as he buried his head in Trevor's chest, re-inserted himself inside Trevor's ass, and began thrusting... "Shhhiiittt.... Umph! Umph! Umph!"

"That's it Daddy... cum for me..." Trevor panted... Bazil was so turned on by Trevor he grabbed Trevor by the face, covered his mouth, with his, slid his tongue in Trevor's mouth, and continued thrusting harder and deeper...

"Umph! Umph! Umph!"

"Mmmmmm.... Mmmmmm.... Mmmmmm...."

"Fuck... Fuck.... Ffffuuuucccckkkk!" Bazil growled as he raised his head and thrust deep inside Trevor and came inside him.

"I love you Daddy..." Trevor breathed as Bazil collapsed on top of him, still inside him. Once Bazil's dick was soft, he slid out of Trevor's ass, pulled off the condom, dropped it in the trash, and snuggled up under Trevor. Bazil and Trevor lay there together, basking in love and orgasms... until Trevor spoke... "You have exquisite taste Baby... this diamond is everythang," he said as he picked up Bazil's hand.

"That would be my wife that has exquisite taste..."

"What? She picked this out?"

"I watched her pick it out and pay for it after we joined the mile high club..."

"Oohh ssshhhiiittt! How was it?"

"It was everythang!"

"Damn... when are you introducing her to your best friend?"

"Soon my love... Be patient..."

"Baby..."

"Yes?"

"We need to get dressed... and we need to talk..."

"Sounds serious..."

"It is..." Trevor said as they got up, got dressed, went into the living room, and sat down...

"Okay... le'me have it," Bazil sighed.

"Here," Trevor said, handing him a Jack Daniels on the rocks and then sitting down with a drink of his own, a folder, and a laptop.

"Damn... that bad huh?"

"Yes Baby... it is..."

"Le'me see that!" Bazil said as he grabbed the folder before Trevor could stop him... "Billie?

This muthafucka? What the fuck does he have to do with this?"

"Baby, please calm down..."

"Answer me Trevor...."

"Billie is Beautiee's husband..." Bazil jumped up from the table and snatched Trevor up out the chair by his throat...

"What the fuck are you telling me Trevor?"

"Baby please... you're scaring me..."

"I'm sorry," Bazil said as he grabbed Trevor into an embrace... "Please tell me Beautiee isn't still married to him..."

"She's not... at least not technically..."

"What do you mean Trevor?" Bazil asked as he sat back down and lowered his voice...

"Remember how he used to always talk about getting even with that Bitch?"

"Beautiee?"

"Yes... Beautiee..."

"I don't understand..."

"They'd only been married for two years before he got arrested..."

"Oh now I remember..."

"He used to always talk about how his Bitch turned on him because she refused to bring him packages..."

"If he truly loved her he would've never asked her to do that... what if she got caught... her life would be over... and for what? Selfish muthafucka... didn't even have enough clout to protect his wife... where was his connect... punk ass... I never liked him anyway... he knew better than to fuck with me..."

"Baby... I know you're upset... but I need you to listen..."

"Okay..."

"Beautiee served him with divorce papers..."

"Good!"

"She filed on grounds of desertion... he refused to sign them..."

"Wait... how you know all this shit?"

"He told me while we were in there..."

"And you didn't think to tell me?"

"Baby... why would I? You couldn't stand his ass and we didn't know who his wife was..."

"You're right... go 'head..."

"So he refused to sign them so Beautiee told him it was in his best interest to let her go without contesting it or things would get ugly..."

"Oh Shit!"

"Yup... so he didn't contest it... but he never signed them either..."

"Is she still married?"

"I don't know," Trevor sighed.

"It doesn't matter... she's my wife now... I don't give a fuck what them damn papers say..."

"Baby the papers say divorce..."

"Okay... I need you to check..."

"I'm already on it... but there's more..."

"Oh God..." Bazil whispered with tears in his eyes. Trevor got up from the table, walked over to Bazil, and held him as he turned on the laptop and played the video surveillance from the hotel. Bazil started to cry as he watched Billie come over to the bar, order a drink, and then bash me in the head with the glass. The bartender tried to intervene but before he could, Billie dragged me from the bar to the elevator, tried to force me inside, and when I refused to go with him he pushed me to the floor and began kicking me in the stomach and ribs. The bartender came around the corner and tried to stop Billie, but Billie laughed, threw him to the floor, and ran through the corridor and out the hotel before anyone could stop him. The bartender helped me up off the floor, walked me back to the bar, and could be seen making me a drink. Before I could take a sip, Bazil sat down beside me. Trevor held Bazil as he continued to cry and they both continued watching the surveillance footage until I went inside the elevator with Bazil...

"You're right... she is beyond her name..." Trevor whispered.

"He needs to die..."

"I know Baby..."

"And it needs to happen NOW!" Bazil growled as he pounded his fist into the table... "Fuck a divorce... she won't need one... lucky for her... she got married again before she became a widow..."

Chapter 15

"Hey my Thirst Quencher," I said as Bazil pulled me into a kiss...

"Mmmmmm...." I moaned...

"Beautiee..."

"I'm thirsty..." I said as I kissed him again...

"We need to talk..."

"But... I'm... thirsty..."

"Beautiee... stop... please... I'm sorry," he said as he took me into the living room.

"What's wrong?" I asked with tears in my eyes...

"I wish I didn't have to do this..."

"Do what Bazil?"

"Wait here... I'll be right back," Bazil said as he got up to go into the kitchen. I sat still on the couch, listening to the ice hitting the glass, and I knew Bazil was making us drinks. When he came back into the living room with the drinks, he wasn't smiling so I knew it was serious... "Here... drink this," he said as he handed me the glass...

"Mmmmmm.... Amaretto Sour... just like the night we met," I sighed as I began drinking...

"You remember," Bazil sighed as he began drinking...

"Yeeesss..." I moaned as I pulled Bazil into a kiss, slipping my tongue in his mouth...

"Beautiee..."

"My Thirst Quencher..."

"Stop..."

"Okay." I was so hurt and so confused...

"Let me explain..." he said as he turned on his lap top. "Come here..." he said as he pulled me close to him and held me...

"Oh God..." I whispered as I started crying... "Where did you get this?"

"That's not important..."

"Why?" I cried as I tried to turn my head away...

"Beautiee..."

"Noooooo!" I screamed...

"I'm here Beautiee..." Bazil whispered with tears in his eyes as he pulled me closer...

"I wish I were dead!"

"Beautiee... please don't say that... he's the one that needs to die... and he will..."

"What did you say?"

"I said he's the one that needs to die... and he will..."

"Bazil... he was my husband..."

"I know..."

"Wait... you know?" I asked as I pulled away from him and sat up...

"Yes Beautiee... I know Billie very well..."

"I'm sorry..." I whispered as I started crying again...

"Beautiee..."

"I love you so much Bazil..."

"Beautiee..."

"Please don't leave me..."

"Beautiee... I made you a promise the night I met you... he said as he started kissing me... "And I made you a promise when we got married..." he said as he continued kissing me... "And I never make a promise I can't keep..."

"You mean... you still want me?"

"I'll... always... want... you..." he said between kisses..."

"I filed for divorce..."

"I know..." Bazil interrupted me with a kiss...

"He... refused... to... sign... the... papers..."

"Stop talking," Bazil commanded as he pulled me into a deep passionate kiss...

"Mmmmmm...." I moaned as he held me and continued kissing me. I wasn't sure what was going on but as long as Bazil wasn't leaving me I didn't care...

"I have something to tell you..."

"Okay..."

"Beautiee... I met Billie when I was in prison..."

"Prison? For what? Drugs? Did you work for Billie?" Oh God..."

"Me? Work for that punk ass muthafucka? Aaaaahhhhhhaaaaaaaa..... Beautiee... let me explain this to you..." he said as he inched towards me... "You see all this?" he asked as he showed me everything in the house.

"Yes."

"I didn't get this by dealing drugs... if I worked for Billie... he would've given you all this and more... but he wasn't man enough to do that... he wasn't man enough to love you... he wasn't man enough to protect you... and by asking you to risk your life to bring him drugs proves he never cared about you... if I knew you before he went to prison... never mind... forget it..."

"What did you do Bazil?"

"Don't ask questions you don't want the answers to Beautiee..."

"What did you do Bazil?"

"As I said, I was in prison with Billie," he explained, ignoring my question... "Trevor was his cell mate. Trevor and I became friends quickly. He was the brother I never had..." I sat listening, watching Bazil drift off smiling. I was still confused but I was relieved to see him smile. "Billie was on some bullshit. He was cool with Trevor but I never trusted that muthafucka. One night I heard all this arguing and yelling so I jumped up to see what was going on..."   I watched Bazil drift off again... this time he wasn't smiling... "Billie made a deal with another inmate... in exchange for drugs... Billie paid him with Trevor..." he whispered as he teared up...

"Come here," I said as I pulled him into a hug and held him.

"I screamed for dear life and got the C.O.'s attention... just in time..." I continued to hold Bazil as he started to cry... "The C.O. had the warden transfer Trevor to my cell for the remainder of his sentence... I was supposed to be in there longer but I got released early because I helped them get Billie...

"Is that why you had to leave in a hurry?"

"Yes. I love him like a brother. He's ride or die."

"I'd like to meet your brother," I sighed.

"That'd be nice..." he said as I kissed him... "Beautiee..."

"Yes my Thirst Quencher," I answered as I started kissing him on his neck...

"Trevor helped me get this..."

"The surveillance?"

"Yes."

"Why?"

"Because I asked him to."

"Why?"

"I made you a promise..."

"I know..."

"I couldn't protect you without knowing what happened..."

"I didn't want to remember..."

"I know Beautiee..."

"I thought I was done with him..."

"You are done with him..."

"How can I be sure?"

"Trust me..." Bazil said as he pulled me into a kiss...

"How did you know... about Billie?" I asked.

"Billie told Trevor all about you when we were in prison... and he also told Trevor he was coming to get revenge..."

"Oh God..." I whispered...

"Trust me Beautiee..." Bazil said as he pushed me back down onto the couch, climbed on top of me, and kissed me deeply. As we lay there kissing, he began to unbutton my blouse, unclasped my bra, and squeezed my breasts. He moved his lips from my mouth, to my neck, and down in between my breasts...

"Bazil..." I breathed as he lifted me up and slid my pants off. He slid his pants down and climbed back on top of me, sliding himself inside me, stroking me... "MmmmMmmm... MmmmMmmm... MmmmMmmm..." I moaned into his mouth as he kissed me, sliding his tongue inside my mouth.

"MmmmMmmmph... MmmmMmmmph... MmmmMmmmph..." he moaned into my mouth... I brought my legs up, grabbed his ass, and pushed him in deeper, letting him know I wanted more... "MmmmMmmm... MmmmMmmm... MmmmMmmm..."

"MmmmMmmmph... MmmmMmmmph... MmmmMmmmph..."

"MmmmMmmm... MmmmMmmm... MmmmMmmm..."

"MmmmMmmmph... MmmmMmmmph... MmmmMmmmph..." We continued to lay there, kissing, until we fell asleep.

Chapter 16

I was in complete awe as I walked in. "Welcome back Mr. Osgood," someone greeted.

"Sam – how many times do I have to tell you…"

"Welcome back Bazil," Sam said as he grabbed Bazil into a hug.

"This is my wife, Beautiee…" Bazil said as he introduced me.

"Wife? What? – I mean – hell – congratulations!" Sam said as he grabbed me into a hug…

"Thanks…" I laughed.

"Oh – my bad – I'm sorry…" he laughed as he let me go…

"Honey… who's this?" she asked playfully as she walked up towards me…

"I'm Bazil's wife, Beautiee…" I smiled.

"Wife? What?" she said as she grabbed me into a hug…

"Ummm… thank you… who are you?" I laughed.

"Oh... I'm sorry.... I'm Joselyn, Sam's wife, Sam's assistant, and Bazil's 2nd assistant," she laughed as she let me go...

"I guess I got my answer..." I laughed.

"Umm... what was the question?" another lady laughed as she walked up to me...

"Well – I was nervous about meeting you all but I can see I had nothing to worry about," I answered.

"Well who are you?" the lady laughed.

"Mother – that's Bazil's new wife, Beautiee," Joselyn answered.

"Oh my God – congratulations – Bazil – you didn't tell me you were seeing anyone!" she laughed as she hugged me...

"I wasn't aware I had to..." Bazil laughed.

"And who are you?" I asked as everyone got quiet...

"Well... since you asked... I'm Sheila. I'm the Chief Financial Officer. This is the Vice President, my son-in-law, Samuel, and this is his wife, my daughter, Joselyn."

"Well it's lovely to meet you Sheila," I said. Bazil stood to the side beaming with pride and I continued with Sheila as I observed another woman walking up on the conversation... "Bazil and I met a little over a week ago...

"A week ago?"

"Yea..."

"Oh I need to hear this... Bazil, we'll be back – we're going for coffee – come with me

Beautiee – you too Joselyn – oh hi MaryJane – this is Beautiee, Bazil's wife – we're going for coffee – you wanna join us?"

"No thank you – nice meeting you though..." she said as she turned to walk towards Bazil and Sam...

"We'll stop in the cafeteria – they make good coffee here," Sheila said as I followed them through the glass doors...

"How do you like your coffee?" Joselyn asked as I sat at one of the tables...

"Hazelnut flavor, hazelnut creamer, light and sweet," I answered.

"Just how Bazil likes 'em..." Sheila laughed as Joselyn walked off to get us coffee... "So tell me how this happened..." Sheila said.

"Well, I met Bazil about a week ago at the Hotel Zero Degrees in Stamford. I was having a drink, he came up to get a drink, we started talking, we hit it off..."

"Hit it off?" Sheila asked...

"Yea..." I answered as I started drifting off...

"Here's your coffee Beautiee," Joselyn said as she sat down with us.

"Beautiee was telling me she met Bazil at the Hotel Zero Degrees a week ago," Sheila said as we started drinking our coffee...

"It happens Ma – you know me and Sam..."

"Yes Joselyn – I know, I know," Sheila laughed.

"Well I don't know – tell me," I laughed.

"I knew I was gonna marry Sam the moment I met him – I didn't know when – but I knew it..." Joselyn answered.

"I had no idea I was getting married – I still can't believe he asked me that night..." I sighed...

"That night? At the hotel?" Sheila asked...

"Well... technically... it wasn't until the next day... before checkout..." I sighed...

"Oh wow..." Joselyn sighed...

"So he met you at the bar... y'all spent the night together... and he proposed the next morning?" Sheila asked...

"Well... technically it was the afternoon... we had a late check out..." I sighed as I drifted off again...

"Well I like you already – you have a nice spirit," Sheila said.

"Awww... thank you..." I said with tears in my eyes...

"You're welcome – so are you going to be working here with Bazil?" she asked.

"Yes I am..." I answered.

"Oh boy – does MaryJane know that?" Joselyn asked.

"I'm sure she does now..." Sheila answered... "And if the doesn't, she goin' learn taday!" she laughed.

"Who's MaryJane?" I asked...

"She's the one who I invited to come get coffee – I knew she wasn't coming anyway – with her stank ass!" Sheila laughed.

"Ma!" Joselyn exclaimed.

"Please Joselyn – you could do her job better – she walks around here like she owns the place… and Bazil…" Sheila said as we continued to sip on our coffee…

"Oh I forgot – I need to get them stats done – le'me run to the bathroom right quick before I miss the deadline," Joselyn said as she darted out of the cafeteria…

"I might as well go to the bathroom – you can make that the 2nd room on the office tour," I laughed.

"Okay – follow me…" Sheila said as she got up and I followed her to the bathroom…

"Oh my God – why?" I heard Joselyn ask…

"She may be nice… for now… until she gets comfortable… then she'll start thinking she runs shit… and I'll have to check her… just like I had to check Janet," I heard MaryJane say. Sheila and I looked at each other and then we both looked back towards the bathroom door…

"You ain't right MaryJane…" Joselyn said.

"Please Joselyn… I've been here for too long to let a Bitch come up in here and knock me outta my position…"

"What position? Your job?"

"That's only part of it…"

"What else is there?"

"She won't last… she may be his wife… for now…"

"What's that supposed to mean?"

"It's only temporary Joselyn," MaryJane answered as she snatched the bathroom door open to exit… and ran right into me…

"Hello MaryJane," I said deliberately as she tried to pass me without excusing herself…

"Oh… Hello Beautiee…" she said…

"Mrs. Osgood," I said, correcting her.

"Excuse me?" MaryJane snapped…

"Please call me Mrs. Osgood," I said as I walked past her, went into the stall, and closed the door. When I came out the stall and went to wash my hands, Sheila spoke…

"Are you okay Beautiee – I mean Mrs. Osgood?"

"Yea… I made it without incident," I answered purposely changing the subject as I washed my hands…

"Ummmmm… I'ma go now…" Joselyn said as she left the bathroom and Sheila followed behind her. I stood there taking my time drying my hands as they spoke on the other side of the door… "Ma… did she hear what MaryJane said?"

"We both did," Sheila answered. I opened the door and walked out into the hallway…

"Sheila, could you please escort me back to my husband's office?"

"Yes Mrs. Osgood – I'll see you later Joselyn," she said as we walked away. I was seething and Sheila knew it, but she didn't say anything as we walked towards Bazil's office...

Chapter 17

"So… you married now huh?"

"Yes I am."

"Does she know about Janet?"

"That's nothing for you to be concerned with…"

"What about me?"

"You'll be fine… as long as you continue to behave…"

"I need to get back to my desk… I'll see you later…" Sheila whispered as she walked away and I continued to listen…

"Who the fuck do you think you're talking to muthafucka?" MaryJane snapped…

"Who the fuck do you think you're talking to?" Bazil growled as he grabbed her throat…

"Bazil… I'm sorry… I can't breathe…"

"You ever speak to me like that again and you won't ever breathe again… are we clear?"

"As clear as we were when you had your dick in my mouth…" she said as she sat down on the sofa and started to unfasten his belt…

"Beautiee... I.... I didn't hear you come in..." Bazil stuttered as I stormed over to the couch, grabbed MaryJane by the back of her hair, and dragged her across the floor towards the door...

"You got 10 seconds to get your ass up and get the fuck off the premises – and let me make myself clear – if I catch your ass back on the premises or anywhere near my husband again – I'll blow your fuckin' head off!" Bazil stood there with his mouth open as Sheila, Sam, Joselyn, and a few other employees watched MaryJane run to her desk, grab her pocket book and keys, and fly out the door... "Joselyn – I need you to clean out your desk!" I said as I walked towards Bazil's office and pushed him inside...

"I'm getting fired? Why?" Joselyn asked as she started to cry...

"Joselyn – I said I need you to clean out your desk!" I repeated as I went into Bazil's office and slammed the door...

"Beautiee... I'm sorry..."

"You fuckin' that Bitch?"

"I was..."

"Who is it?" I snapped...

"Joselyn..."

"Come in Joselyn..." I said as I looked at Bazil and Joselyn came inside, sat on the sofa, and put a box of personal items on the floor... "Joselyn – since MaryJane no longer works here – we need a personal assistant – I'm offering the position to you... if you're interested..." I said as I sat down beside her and took her hand...

"Thank you Mrs. Osgood..." she breathed as she sighed with relief...

"You're welcome – I'll need you to start immediately – that's why I asked you to clean out your desk...

"Oooohhh... okay...."

"Since you'll be working for both of us you're going to have additional responsibilities... so we'll make your raise retro-active starting today – Bazil, can you take care of the paperwork so I can get settle in?"

"Yes Beautiee," Bazil answered as he went out into the hall...

"Bazil – is my wife getting fired?" Sam asked.

"No Sam – but she won't be working for you any longer..."

"What happened Bazil?"

"My wife fired MaryJane... and promoted your wife..." Bazil answered as he smiled...

"Oh shit!"

"I'm on my way to get her paperwork started – my wife instructed me to make her raise effective today..."

"I love your wife!" Sam exclaimed...

"I love her too..." Bazil said...

"So MaryJane is gone for good?"

"I'm surprised you didn't hear about it..."

"Hear about what?"

"Your wife didn't tell you?"

"My wife was too upset…"

"Well… MaryJane forgot her place… she spoke outta turn… and my wife heard what she said…"

"Oh shit! What the fuck happened?"

"My wife snatched the Bitch by her hair… dragged her across the floor… and told her she had 10 seconds to get the fuck off the premises!" Bazil laughed…

"What?! And I missed it?!"

"You missed it…"

"Bazil… you're not worried?"

"Fuck her…" Bazil laughed…

"Damn Bazil… that's fucked up…"

"She fucked up…"

"Bazil… she could file a lawsuit for wrongful termination…"

"And she could also be permanently terminated…" Bazil said as Joselyn and I came out into the hallway…

"Hey Sam – did Bazil tell you the news?" I asked as I walked past them with Joselyn…

"Yes he did – congratulations baby," Sam said as he pulled his wife into a kiss, causing her to drop the box… "Sorry baby – le'me get that for you – where are we going?"

"We're going to your wife's new office," I answered.

"Yes Maam," Sam said as he walked towards MaryJane's old office...

"Mrs. Osgood," I corrected."

"Yes Mrs. Osgood," Sam acknowledged as Bazil headed over to payroll and I walked to Joselyn's new office with Sam...

"Oh my God – is everything okay?" Sheila yelled as she came running into the office...

"Yes Mother," Joselyn answered.

"Isn't this MaryJane's office?" Sheila asked...

"She no longer works here," I answered...

"Ooookkkaaayyyy...." Sheila said as she backed out of the office...

"Joselyn – please come see me as soon as you get settled – Sam – I need you to call a staff meeting asap!"

"Yes Mrs. Osgood," Sam said as he hurried down the hall to get Bazil...

"Joselyn – where do they hold staff meetings at?"

"They usually hold them in conference room 1," she answered as she continued unpacking her box and setting up her new desk..."

"Thank you Joselyn," I said as I hurried to the conference room...

"Hey Beautiee..." Bazil said nervously as I walked over to him... "Are you getting settled in okay?"

"Thank you all for coming," I said as Sheila, Joselyn, and other employees came into the conference room. "Sam, could you close the door please?"

"Yes Mrs. Osgood," Sam said as he went to the door and closed it...

"For those of you who don't know me, I'm Mrs. Osgood." I watched for a moment as some of the employees started whispering... "I know you're all shocked... I'm still in shock myself," I said as I wrapped my arm around Bazil and stood beside him. "I'll be working alongside my husband and I will also be making personnel changes as I deem necessary," I continued. I watched again as some of the employees started whispering... "Having said that, I have two announcements," I continued... "First ‑ effective immediately – MaryJane LaRue no longer works here – furthermore, she is not to be near or on the premises..." I watched again as some of the employees whispered and others gasped... "Second – effective immediately – Joselyn Logan has been promoted to our Personal Assistant." I watched, listened, and observed as all the employees got up to congratulate Joselyn...

"My baby!" Sheila yelled...

"'Bout damn time..."

"Girl – I'm so happy for you..."

"Yes Honey!"

"Congratulations!"

"Thank you, thank you, thank you..." Joselyn said in between hugs. I watched as the employees went to sit back down...

"So let me tell you a little bit about myself. I've always been a writer. Growing up in foster care comes with a great deal of challenges, and writing was how I dealt with them." I watched and observed as everyone got eerily quiet, eager to hear what I had to say – and it made me smile. "As a child, I would write songs, poems, and essays. When it was time for me to graduate from elementary school, the Principal asked us to write an essay about our experiences and I wrote an essay about the way they teased me when I had eye surgery and had to wear prisms on my glasses – I even wrote a song about it to help me cope." Some of the employees looked at each other nodding and shaking their heads as I continued... "I was surprised when the principal told me my essay was chosen to be read at the Graduation Assembly and I sang the song I wrote to the Assembly. I continued writing through high school and college – partly because it was required – but mostly because I really enjoyed it and still do. Along with writing, I was also reading - in fact, I read so much my grandmother used to yell at me when I went grocery shopping with her because I'd always read the labels on the canned foods and desserts before I put them in the cart." Everyone burst into laughter. I waited for them all to calm down before I continued. "As

I got older, I would read books, critique them, and change the ending by saying 'I would have said this, I would have done that. My friends would always tell me you should write a book and I would always say one day – and one day finally came. I published my 1st book with a vanity publisher in 2003, I made mistakes, and I learned what I didn't like about vanity publishers. Since writing is in my blood, rather than give up on publishing, I went to writing expos, author signings, etc., and learned some more. The turning point for me was when I had a one-on-one with Michael Baisden who sat with me, gave me advice, and took out his tape recorder to make a note when he thought I had a good idea. I turned my first book into a 5-book series, and I was ready to publish them but I knew I wasn't going back to vanity publishing so I reached out to David L. at Total Package Publications. He referred me to selfpublishing.com, and they gave me step-by-step instructions on the entire process from purchasing your own ISBN numbers to starting your own publishing company, so I started Beautiful Publications in 2014 and published my series myself." Bazil was so proud standing there. The room was quiet until Joselyn raised her hand… "Yes Joselyn?"

"Where can we buy your books?"

"You can't."

"Why not?"

"Because you work for me so I won't sell them to you – but what I will do is give you all copies for your review if you'd like…"

"Oooohhhh…" all the employees said in unison.

"Now that you know a lil' something about me I'm looking forward to getting to know a lil' something about you too – in time – right now though, I need to get settled and get up to speed – Joselyn – I need you to clear my husband's calendar for the rest of the day – Sam I need you to handle whatever comes up – we'll see everyone tomorrow…" I said as I took Bazil by the hand and we went to his office…

"Come here Beautiee…" Bazil said as he pulled me into a kiss… "I'm so proud of how you took charge and handled business today…" Bazil said as I tried to pull away from him…" Beautiee… please… I didn't mean for that to happen…"

"I know… let go of me…"

"Is that what you want?"

"Yes Bazil…"

"Okay… if that's what you want…" he said as he let me go and sat down on the sofa…

"How many times did you fuck her on this couch Bazil?"

"Beautiee… please…"

"Answer me Bazil…"

"A few months…" Bazil whispered as he put his head in his hands…

"I was so happy when I got up this morning – I couldn't wait to come here – I was so happy that everyone started to like me..." I said as I started crying...

"Beautiee... please don't cry... I'm sorry..."

"Let me finish Bazil..."

"Okay..." he said with tears in his eyes...

"Sheila took me to the cafeteria with Joselyn and we had coffee – I was telling them how we met and you proposed the next day..." I said as I began to smile. Bazil started to smile before I continued... "Joselyn was telling me how she knew she was going to marry Sam the moment she met him..."

"Aww... that's beautiful... he loves her as much as I love you..."

"That isn't possible," I laughed.

"You're right," Bazil laughed...

"Anyway... Joselyn said she had to finish her stats so she went to the ladies room... Sheila and I finished our coffee and I said we might as well go too – I even joked about her making it part of the office tour..."

"Sounds like you hit it off..."

"That's exactly what I told her about me and you," I said as I smiled. Bazil took my hand as I continued... "Sheila told me in the cafeteria that MaryJane walked around like she owned the place... and you..."

"Sheila never liked MaryJane..."

"After what we heard I understand why she didn't like her..."

"What?" Bazil interrupted...

"When we got to the ladies room we heard MaryJane talking to Joselyn... about me..."

"Oh hell no..." Bazil whispered...

"She told Joselyn that she worked here too long to let a Bitch knock her out of her position..."

"And Sheila heard this conversation?"

"We both did..."

"Did she say anything else?"

"She told Joselyn as soon as I got comfortable she was going to have to check me... like she had to check Janet... who's Janet Bazil?" Bazil didn't answer me right away. His eyes turned to slits and the vein in his neck started twitching. His blood was boiling and I could feel the anger coming from him...

"Janet was my first wife - but what else did she say?"

"I'm afraid to tell you Bazil..."

"Beautiee please... I'm not going to hurt you..."

"I know you won't hurt me... but you might hurt her..."

"Beautiee... what... did... she... say?"

"She said I may be your wife for now... but it's only temporary..."

"And Sheila heard this entire conversation?"

"Yes."

"I need to speak to Sheila immediately," Bazil said as he went to get up...

"You need to speak to me right now Bazil..."

"You're right... I'm sorry..."

"Sheila walked me back to your office... and she heard some of what MaryJane said to you before she walked away..."

"Oh God – please tell me she didn't hear that Bitch say she had my dick in her mouth..." Bazil moaned...

"She didn't hear that – but I did – remember?"

"I'm sorry... I wish I never met that Bitch – she better be glad it was you that dragged her ass outta here and not me..."

"You would've been in jail Bazil..."

"I've been there before..."

"Where would that leave me Bazil?"

"You're right... I'm sorry..."

"Everything was going so good until that Bitch forgot her place – and I had to put her back in it..."

"I'm so sorry..."

"When I heard her say she had your dick in her mouth I lost it - I could've killed her - I meant what I said Bazil - if I catch her anywhere near you again... I'll make good on that promise..."

"I know..."

"You know?"

"I saw how you took care of business... and so did everyone else..."

"I'm not proud of that Bazil – that's not how my first day was supposed to be..."

"Yes it was..."

"Bazil!"

"Beautiee... listen to me..." Bazil said as he took my face in his hands and kissed me... "Trust me... after what I witnessed today in your first meeting as my wife, my business partner – you have their admiration – and you have their respect..." he said as he continued to kiss me...

"Bazil..." I interrupted...

"Yes Beautiee..." he breathed as he kissed me again...

"What happened to Janet?" Bazil let go of me and stared out the window for a few moments before he answered me...

"She died." I didn't ask any more questions. I got up, left Bazil sitting on the sofa, and went to Joselyn's office...

"Joselyn – please come with me," I said as I waited for her to get up...

"Yes Mrs. Osgood," she said as she followed me back to Bazil's office...

"Close the door Joselyn," I said as Bazil looked back and forth between the two of us...

"Is something wrong Mrs. Osgood?" Joselyn asked.

"Something's definitely wrong Joselyn – I need you to get me an interior designer – I want this office done from top to bottom – I want new lighting – I want calm soothing colors – and I also want this wall gone so my desk will fit in here along with my husband's – I want his name on this door and my name on the other door – are you getting this Joselyn?"

"I gotchu you – go 'head," she laughed.

"You wanna add anything Bazil?" I asked.

"As long as I don't walk into a women's lounge you can do whatever you want," Bazil laughed.

"Don't worry Bazil – oh – before I forget – Joselyn?"

"Yes Mrs. Osgood?"

"This fuckin' couch has got to go – tonight!"

"Yes Mrs. Osgood – Sam · I need your help!" she yelled out to her husband as Bazil and I left.

Chapter 18

"What's next?" Bazil asked as we got into the car...

"You're going to feed me..." I answered seductively...

"As you wish..." Bazil said seductively as we sped off. When we got home I couldn't get in the door fast enough... and neither could he... "Where do you think you're going?" Bazil asked as I tried to run upstairs...

"I was planning on going back to bed," I laughed...

"In that case... let me help you..." Bazil said as he picked me up in his arms and carried me upstairs into the bedroom...

"I could get used to this..." I breathed as he lay me down on the bed and began undressing me...

"So..." he whispered in my ear... "How hungry are you?"

"I'm starving..." I breathed as he began sucking my earlobe...

"Which appetite shall I satisfy first?" he breathed as he slid out of his clothes...

"As long as I'm full when you're done... I don't care..." I breathed...

"As you wish..." he breathed as he dove in to eat...

"Oooohhh...." I moaned... "I thought I was hungry..."

"I'm hungry too..." he growled as he sucked, licked, and slurped...

"Oh Bazil... that feels so fuckin' good... shit..."

"Damn Beautiee... you're ready to cum..." he said as he slid two fingers inside...

"Bazziilll!" I screamed as I grabbed his head and my legs trembled...

"Mmmmmm..." Bazil moaned as my pussy quenched his thirst... "Are you still hungry?"

"Yeeesss...."

"Good..." he breathed as he thrust himself inside me...

"Bazil..."

"Beautiee..."

"Bazil..."

"Beautiee..."

"Just... like... that... fuck!"

"Is this what you want?" he growled as he threw my legs up on his shoulders...

"Yes! Yes! Yes!" I screamed...

"Uggh! Uggh! Uggh!" he growled as he came behind me, collapsing on top of me...

"Damn that was good..." I breathed...

"Yes... it... was..." Bazil said between kisses...

"I'm really hungry Bazil..."

"I know... I'll get up and make you breakfast... just let me lay here inside you..." he said between kisses...

"Okay..." I breathed as I kissed him back... until we both fell back to sleep...

"Yo! Bazil! You home?"

"Bazil..." I said as I jumped up...

"Huh?" he answered sleepily...

"Someone's at the door..."

"Yo Bazil! Open the door – this shit's heavy!"

"Oh shit – that's Troy!" Bazil said as he jumped up out of bed, grabbed his robe, and flew downstairs to open the door...

"Why the hell didn't you answer the door man - didn't you hear me?" Troy said as he put the bags on the counter...

"Oh so you are home – why aren't you at work?" she asked as she came inside...

"Umm... Hi..." I said as I came downstairs in one of Bazil's robes...

"Oh shit – damn Bazil – my bad – sorry!" Troy laughed.

"You must be Troy," I said as I went to take his hand...

"Nice to meet you... umm... Bazil... who is this?"

"I'm his wife, Beautiee," I smiled.

"Wife? Since when?" she asked.

"Since Sunday," Bazil answered as he pulled me into a kiss...

"'Bout damn time you found somebody – you could'a told us you were dating – we would'a thrown yall an engagement party," she said.

"I don't know you yet – but I like you," I laughed...

"I'm Keisha, Troy's wife – so how long we're y'all dating?"

"Keisha?" I asked.

"Yes?"

"What's in the bag?"

"Ohhh – we always look out for Bazil 'cause he don't cook – we got Buffalo wings, potato skins, garlic bread with cheese, beef patties, and turkey clubs..."

"Thank God – I'm starving!" I said as I started pulling food out the bag and unwrapping it...

"Damn Bazil – you gotta start cooking!" Troy laughed.

"I will... now that I have reason to..." Bazil said as he pulled me into a kiss...

"Aww... don't they remind you of us Babe?" Keisha asked...

"Nope," Troy said between bites... "'Cause I would'a fed you..."

"Shut the fuck up Troy!" Bazil laughed.

"So how long have you been dating?" Keisha asked.

"We haven't..." I answered.

"So y'all met and got married?"

"Basically..." I laughed.

"Are you serious?" Keisha asked...

"Yes..."

"Bazil... what'd you do to her?" Keisha asked as Troy bust out laughing...

"I loved her..." he answered as he kissed me again...

"Damn!" Troy yelled. We sat there and continued to eat without speaking until all the food was finished... and then Keisha spoke...

"Okay Beautiee – what happened – I know he loved you – that's what Bazil does – but what happened?"

"We met at the Hotel Zero Degrees in Stamford. I was sitting at the bar having a drink and he came and sat next to me. I asked him who he was and he said, 'I'm your Thirst Quencher.'"

"Oh Damn!" Keisha gasped. Troy gave Bazil a pound as I continued...

"He took a sip of my drink, kissed me, and put his tongue in my mouth..." Bazil sat there smiling as Keisha and Troy both had their mouths open... "He asked me to go with him to his room and I did..."

"Oh hell no – girl you crazy!" Keisha yelled.

"Really Keisha?" Troy asked as he raised an eyebrow...

"Shut up Troy – go 'head Beautiee..."

"Na... I wanna know what happened with you two!" I laughed.

"We met at a party..." Keisha answered...

"And?" Troy asked...

"And I went home with Troy that night – you happy now?" Keisha laughed...

"So you're as crazy as I am," I laughed...

"I guess so... what happened when you got to the room?"

"We took a shower... Bazil washed my hair... and then we went to bed and he held me until I fell asleep..."

"That's what's up!" Troy said as he gave Bazil another pound...

"That's it?" Keisha asked...

"We had breakfast in the morning – at first I didn't remember what happened or where I was – but once I saw Bazil I remembered..." I answered, smiling. Bazil was smiling too. "Bazil proposed to me after we had breakfast..." I sighed.

"You must be the one..." Keisha said.

"She is..." Bazil said.

"So where'd you get married?" Keisha asked.

"Vegas."

"Damn Bazil – you couldn't let her get away huh?" Troy asked...

"Nope," Bazil answered.

"So you just got home?" Keisha asked.

"We got home yesterday," I sighed.

"I still can't believe it..." Keisha said...

"Neither can I..." I sighed...

"So are you going to be working with Bazil?" Troy asked.

"Yes she is..." Bazil answered for me... "She met everyone earlier today..."

"How'd that go?" Keisha asked...

"I fired someone, promoted someone, and held my first staff meeting..." I answered matter-of-factly...

"What?! Damn – you went in like that – what she do?"

"Well..." I started to say as I noticed Bazil was getting uncomfortable... "I went to the ladies room and before I could open the door she was in there talkin' about she been there too long to let a Bitch knock her outta her position and as soon as I got comfortable she was gonna check me..."

"Oh hell no – I'da put fire to her ass right in the fuckin' ladies room..."

"It gets better..."

"Oh shit – what happened?"

"The Chief Financial Officer heard what she said too..."

"She's a dumb Bitch!" Troy yelled as I continued...

"So Sheila walked me to Bazil's office…" Bazil's eyes got really big as I continued… "and the Bitch was in there…"

"Oh shit!" Keisha yelled…

"So… I snatched the Bitch by her hair, dragged her across the floor to the door… and told her she had 10 seconds to get the fuck up and get the fuck off the premises!" I laughed.

"I know that's right!" Keisha laughed.

"Yo! Beautiee's gangsta!" Troy laughed.

"Yes she is…" Bazil laughed.

"She might sue – you better be careful…" Keisha said…

"And she might not make it to court…" I laughed…

"I like your ass!" Keisha laughed…

"I like your ass too!" I laughed as we hugged. Bazil and Troy looked at each other and smiled.

"So who got promoted?" Keisha asked.

"Sam's wife, Joselyn," I answered.

"Who's Sam?" Troy asked.

"My CEO," Bazil answered.

"Damn! I like your ass too!" Troy laughed as we hugged.

"Bazil – you ain't mad?" Keisha asked.

"'Not at all," Bazil smiled… "She disrespected my wife… nobody comes for Beautiee… but me…" he smiled mischievously…

"Awww shit!" Troy laughed.

"So what's up for the rest of the day?" Keisha asked...

"I'm thinking about going back to bed... now that I ate..." I yawned.

"Still hungry?" Bazil asked seductively...

"I always have an appetite..." I answered seductively...

"Alright – we'll go – but we may come back later – if that's alright..." Keisha said as we all got up from the table and walked towards the door...

"Y'all are welcome here anytime..." I yawned as I hugged Keisha, hugged Troy, and went upstairs...

"Congratulations Bazil – don't fuck this up!" Troy said...

"I won't – love y'all..." Bazil said as he hugged them...

"Love you to Bazil... later," Keisha said as they left, Bazil locked the door, and went into the library...

"I got a bad feeling Troy..." Keisha said as they headed towards their house...

"Damn Keisha... I thought you liked her!"

"I do... I just got a bad feeling..."

"Bazil? Bazil? Bazil? Le'me go see where the hell he is!" I said out loud as I walked downstairs and went towards the library. I stood there for a few moments and watched Bazil sleeping in the lounge chair with a copy of my book opened across his lap before I went back upstairs and went to sleep.

Chapter 19

I woke up to the smell of coffee... and biscuits... "Damn that smells good..." I said out loud as I got up to go downstairs and into the kitchen...

"Beautiee... you're awake..." Bazil said as he pulled me into a kiss...

"Mmmmmm... taste's good..." I said after tasting butter on his lips...

"Sit down Beautiee..." Bazil said as he turned to finish preparing breakfast. I picked up my coffee and enjoyed the hazelnut flavor as I drank slowly. Bazil placed the plates on the table and it was a sight for hungry eyes - fruit salad, sweet potatoes, cheddar omelets, buttermilk biscuits, bacon, and sausage.

"Bazil..." I sighed...

"I promised you I'd cook you breakfast..." he said as he sat at the table with me... and then picked up my fork...

"Bazil... I need that..."

"No you don't..." he said as he used the fork to cut a piece of my omelet, put it on the fork, and bring it to my mouth... "Open..."he said. I opened my mouth as Bazil gently placed the fork in...

"Ohhhh my God!" I moaned as I tasted the omelet... "Damn that's good..."

"I'm glad you're enjoying it..." Bazil said seductively. I picked up his fork, cut a piece of his omelet, and brought the fork to his mouth. Bazil opened his mouth, I placed the fork in, and watched as Bazil chewed and swallowed. When he picked up his coffee and took a sip, the sight of his Adam's apple moving up and down as he swallowed turned me on immensely... "You're enjoying this aren't you?"

"Yeeesss...." I breathed. We continued eating without speaking. After we finished our food, Bazil got up from the table, picked up the dishes, and placed them in the sink. When he came back to the table, he took my hand for me to get up from the table but I resisted...

"Come with me Beautiee..."

"Sit in front of me... on the table..." I commanded. Bazil slid himself in front of me and stood there for a few moments... "Get on the table..." I repeated. Bazil hopped up on the table and started to untie his robe... "Let me..." I said as I moved his hands away from the belt on his robe. I put my head between his legs and spread them with my hands as I moved in closer...

"Beautiee..." Bazil moaned as he began running his hands through my hair. I untied the belt and Bazil's dick came towards my mouth fully erect. I opened my mouth and took his dick in slowly. Bazil began to push my head further down his shaft until his dick was in my mouth completely...

"Mmmmm...." I moaned on Bazil's dick so he could feel the vibration...

"Beautiee... yyyeeesss..." Bazil moaned as I pulled my mouth off his dick, sucking as I did so. Bazil gently guided my mouth back onto his dick, inching himself closer to the edge of the table, making it easier for me to take him back in my mouth. Bazil kept his hands on my head, allowing me to suck his dick to my heart's content... as well as his... "Yeesss... suck it..." he moaned as I enjoyed pleasing him... "I'm cumming... oh shit... uuuggghhh!" he growled as he came in my mouth. I continued sucking gently as Bazil played in my hair... "Let's go upstairs..." he breathed...

"Okay..." I sighed as he got down off the table and held out his hand to take mine. I took his hand, got up from the chair, and Bazil led me upstairs to the bedroom...

Twisted Beautiee

<u>Twisted Beautiee Tree</u>

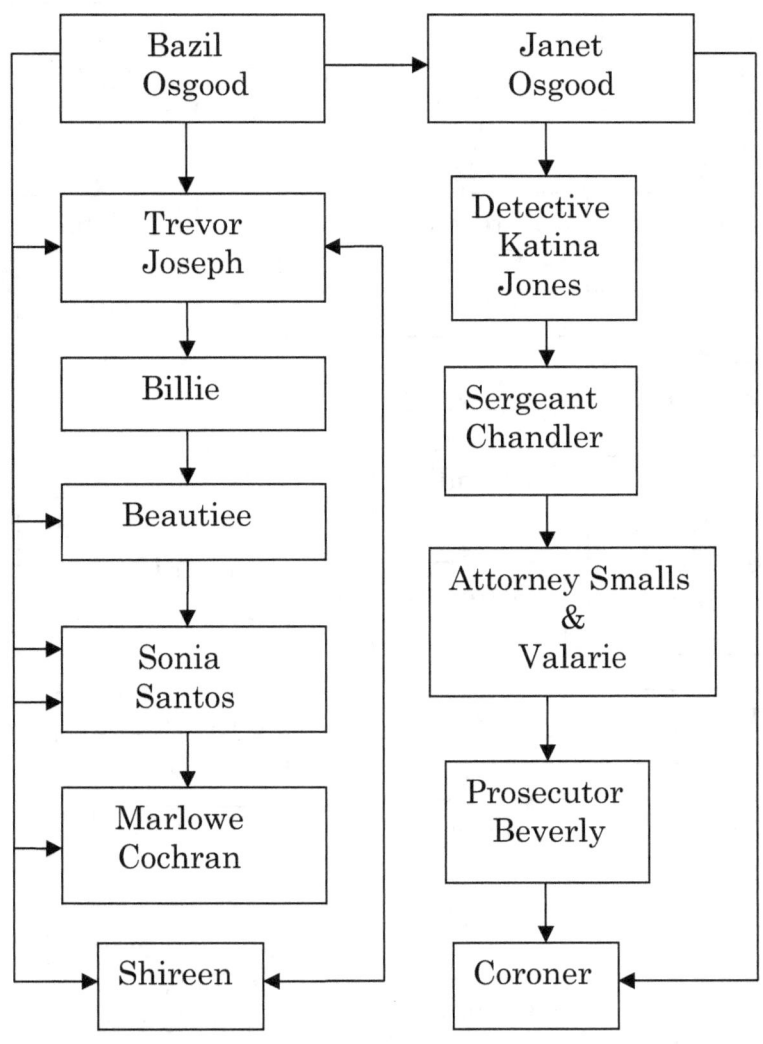

<u>Twisted Beautiee Tree</u>

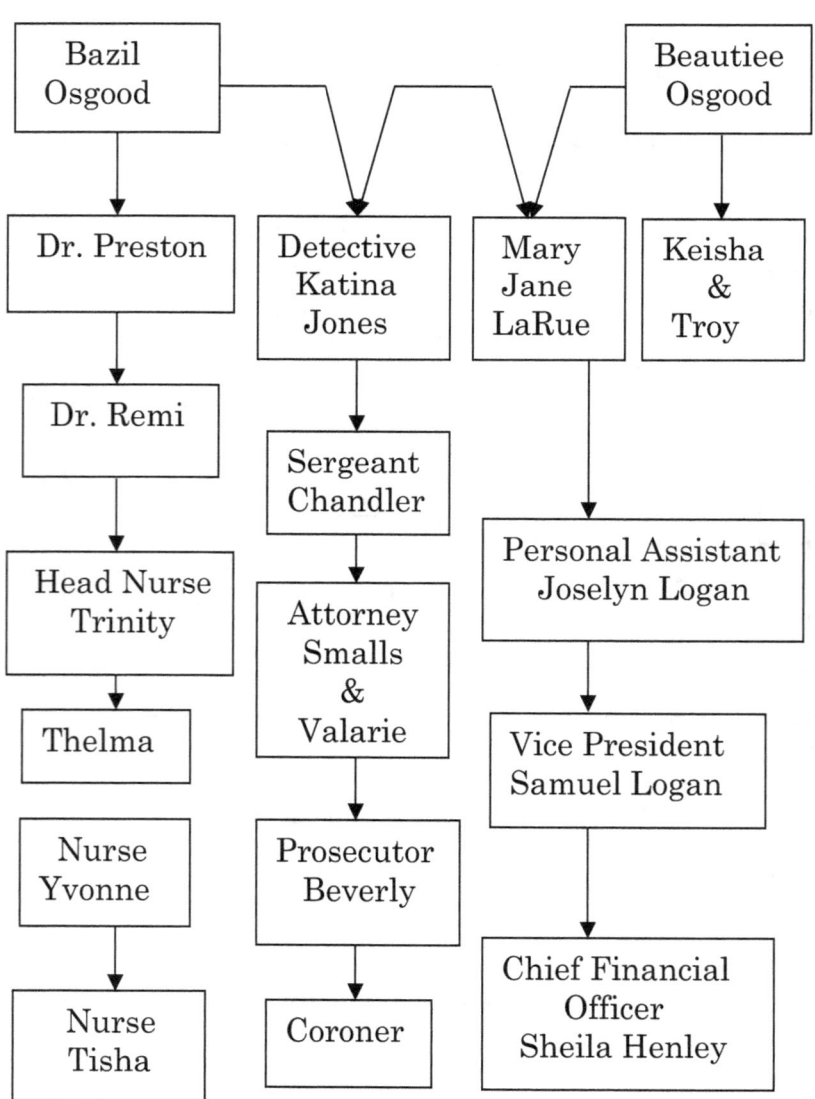

www.ingramcontent.com/pod-product-compliance
Lightning Source LLC
Chambersburg PA
CBHW072108170626
46813CB00004B/1483